BOOK HAVEN

AND OTHER CURIOSITIES

MARK ALLAN GUNNELLS

Let the world know:
#IGotMyCLPBook!

Crystal Lake Publishing
www.CrystalLakePub.com

Copyright © 2019 By Crystal Lake Publishing
All Rights Reserved

Property of Crystal Lake Publishing

Be sure to sign up for our newsletter and receive
a free eBook: http://eepurl.com/xfuKP

ISBN: 978-1-68454-546-9

Layout:
Lori Michelle—www.theauthorsalley.com

Proofread by:
Amanda Shore
Paula Limbaugh

SET YOUR
IMAGINATION
FREE!

OTHER TITLES BY MARK ALLAN GUNNELLS:

Flowers in a Dumpster

Where the Dead Go to Die (co-authored with Aaron Dries)

Curtain Call

The Quarry

The Cult of Ocasta

Deviations from the Norm

Asylum

Fort

Companions in Ruin

Sequel

Tales from the Midnight Shift

Ghosts in the Attic

October Roses

Dark Treats

Halloween House of Horrors

Outcast

The Summer of Winters

Welcome to the Graveyard

Dog Days o' Summer (co-authored with James Newman)

#MakeHalloweenScaryAgain (part of Random House's *Halloween Carnival Vol. 1)*

OTHER SHORT STORY COLLECTIONS
BY CRYSTAL LAKE PUBLISHING

Darker Days by Kenneth W. Cain

Dead Reckoning and Other Stories by Dino Parenti

Things You Need by Kevin Lucia

The Ghost Club: Newly Found Tales of Victorian Terror by William Meikle

Ugly Little Things: Collected Horrors by Todd Keisling

Whispered Echoes by Paul F. Olson

The Dark at the End of the Tunnel by Taylor Grant

Where You Live by Gary McMahon

Tricks, Mischief and Mayhem by Daniel I. Russell

Samurai and Other Stories by William Meikle

Stuck On You and Other Prime Cuts by Jasper Bark

TABLE OF CONTENTS

For Bradbury and Serling, who taught me so much about the magical art of storytelling.

BOOK HAVEN

Article from the Columbia, South Carolina online news source, **The State:**

Three weeks have passed since the event which has come to be known around the world as "the Wipe", and authorities are still no closer to determining who is responsible for creating the virus that deleted the digital files of all fictional works of literature from every online database. The virus was insidiously designed to erase all downloaded copies, and the world's leading computer experts have been unsuccessful at recovering any of the files.

In a press conference held yesterday in front of the White House, President Bachman said, "This is a clear-cut case of cyber terrorism. The virus targeted only literature files, which is a great blow to both art and history, but the ramifications of this are even more terrifying. What would stop these terrorists from targeting medical records or classified military documents or birth certificates or personal financial information? It is imperative that we make discovering and apprehending those responsible for this heinous act a top priority."

Since the production of physical books was discontinued nearly a century ago, printed volumes have become obsolete relics relegated to museums. The price of physical books on the secondhand market have skyrocketed following the Wipe.

During his press conference on the matter, the president also confirmed that the Senate is forming a subcommittee to formulate a plan to deal with the literary crisis here at home while the U.S. government communicates with other world leaders to coordinate efforts. Unconfirmed rumors speculate that several facilities all over the country will be formed to focus on the problem, including one right here in Columbia, South Carolina . . .

THE LIBRARY

THE RAIN SPLATTERED down from the gray clouds, languid and dispirited, as if to match Paul Nelson's mood.

He pulled the car into the parking lot of the Library just as his cell chirped in his ear. He knew who the caller was without checking the display on the dash; he let it go to voicemail. A warning light informed him the car was running low on juice, so he parked in one of the recharging spaces, knowing the engine would be topped off by the time he left work. One of the perks of having a government job was that he didn't have to pay for the electricity.

And on days like this, he needed to remind himself the job did come with perks. It wasn't all gloom and disappointment.

Just keep telling yourself that until you finally start to believe it.

With a sigh, Paul cut the engine and sat in silence, staring through the windshield at the squat, gray, rectangular building where he worked. The nondescript, industrial architecture of a government facility. The official name for the facility was the *Southeastern Institute for Acquisition and Restoration of Literature*, but everyone always called it the Library. Succinct, both appropriate and sadly ironic at the same time.

The rain became a downpour, as if trying to dissuade Paul from getting out of the car and going inside. Weary, he wished he could just go home, but it wasn't an option. He still had his duties.

Paul grabbed his satchel from the passenger's seat, slipped out of the car, and sprinted to the building. Though the distance was only a few feet, the heavy shower drenched him by the time he reached the door. He stepped into the vestibule, dripping onto the threadbare carpet. He shook himself off and took a steadying breath before walking through the large, open area, which made up most of the building.

The space was divided up into twenty-four cubicles, a dozen on each side with an aisle running down the center to the offices at the back. He could feel eyes tracking him from the open doorways of the cubicles, but he hoped his gruff expression and purposeful walk would discourage anyone from speaking to him.

The door to Alison Wyatt's office was shut, for which Paul was grateful. She'd been calling and messaging him for the past half hour, and he just wasn't in the mood to talk to her. Not yet. Someone in the office was sure to let her know Paul had returned, but maybe he could sneak in a few more minutes of peace before having to endure her third degree.

But this wasn't to be. While still several steps from his office, he spotted Alison emerging from the restroom to the right. She called his name and started his way, but he pretended not to hear and hurried into his office, closing the door behind him. Chances were slim this would deter Alison, but he could always hope.

Alison stopped abruptly when Paul went into his office and shut the door. She knew he'd seen her, and she knew he'd heard her. This combined with his radio silence since the auction ended did not bode well. She considered giving him a little time to sulk but then thought better of it. They had a job to do, and when setbacks were encountered, it was even more important to rally.

A few quick strides brought her to the office door. She raised her hand to knock, stopped herself, and instead twisted the knob to let herself in. She saw Paul dropping into the chair behind his desk, and at the sight of her, he let a shuddering breath escape his lips. The very sound of exasperation.

"Come in," he said with a sarcastic lilt.

Alison ignored his tone. Two could play at that game. "So," she said, closing the door and taking the empty chair across the desk from him. "I take it you were not successful in procuring the copy of *Fried Green Tomatoes at the Whistle Stop Cafe* at the auction?"

Paul's expression gave her the answer before he spoke. "I didn't even get a chance to bid."

"What? I thought the Subcommittee had authorized you to spend up to five thousand dollars?"

"They did, and the first bid was fifteen thousand."

Alison whistled softly. "That's a serious private collector with some deep pockets. Anyone we know?"

"Never saw him before. Couldn't have been more than twenty-five years old, but he wore an ill-fitting suit and looked damn uncomfortable in it. Like a kid wearing his father's clothes."

Alison leaned forward with her elbows on her knees, intrigued. "Do we know who he was representing?"

"I checked the registration roster, and it had him listed as Bo Havisham from something called LitCorp. I got on the 'net but couldn't find anything on him or the company. *Nothing*."

"Hmm, so it seems we have a new player in town."

"And one who, as you said, has some pretty deep pockets."

Alison remained silent, deciding whether she wanted to continue. Paul had seemed depressed for months now, and today's failure only made it worse. Perhaps she should let sleeping dogs lie, as the old saying went.

No! Damn it, you're not his mother. You shouldn't have to coddle him. He's a professional, so he needs to suck it up and move forward. It's your job as his assistant to keep him on track.

"Paul, I know you're feeling let down, and I hate to add to your disappointment . . . "

"Let me guess, you have another bit of bad news for me?"

"More than one, actually."

⎯⌇⎰⌇⎯

Paul groaned and grasped the edge of his desk, bracing himself for the next blow. He didn't need more bad news, not with his mood already darker than the rainclouds outside. Some things couldn't be avoided though.

"What is it?"

"Well," Alison said in her typical dispassionate

tone, "I'll start with the biggie. You remember Evelyn Mills?"

Of course Paul remembered Ms. Mills—an old woman with a complete set of *Oz* books in her possession, which she said had belonged to her great-grandmother. He'd spoken to her only yesterday.

"What about her?" he asked, a dread settling over him like ashes.

"She contacted me while you were out and said she's no longer willing to sell."

Paul slammed his open palms onto the desktop, causing Alison to flinch. "I don't believe it; this was nearly a done deal. We were negotiating the price."

"She said she just couldn't part with such a precious family heirloom."

"Precious? Half of them were mildewing in the basement, and the other half had decorative plates sitting on top of them in a china cabinet."

"I suspect there's more to it."

"Why do you say that?"

"Because we were doing a video chat, and I couldn't help but notice she wore what looked like a brand new pair of diamond earrings and a matching choker. Seems unlikely a woman on a fixed income like Ms. Mills would be able to afford that type of extravagant jewelry."

"Could be fakes?"

"Could be, or it could be—"

"Book Hounds," Paul spat.

"That would be my guess. They made her a better offer."

Paul slapped the desk again, heedless of the stinging in his hands. Book Hounds had become the bane of his professional existence, and to think he'd once considered them beneath his concern. When the Libraries had first been founded by the Senate Subcommittee for Literary Reconstruction, little competition had existed, and resources had been ample. However, times had changed in the two years since the Wipe, and Book Hounds now considered the Libraries beneath *their* concern.

"I've got to schedule a meeting with Senator Kelley again to talk about our budget."

Alison sighed. "Seriously, you never make any headway with him. I don't know why you want to keep beating your head against that particular brick wall."

"I've got to make him understand as long as they keep slashing our acquisitions budget then we're going to keep losing books. If they approve me to spend two thousand dollars on an acquisition, the Book Hounds sneak in and offer two thousand one hundred and steal it right from under us. Then they turn around and sell it to a private collector for five thousand dollars and make a hefty profit. There's no way we can win in that dynamic."

"Paul, I think Senator Kelley and the entire subcommittee understands that, but they see the restoration department as being more cost effective."

Paul grimaced as if he'd just tasted something sour. "Restoration was only ever supposed to be a temporary stop-gap measure; the Libraries were founded with acquisition as their main goal."

"Times have changed," she said, mimicking his earlier thoughts. "Restoration is much cheaper than acquisition."

"Well, you get what you pay for. A bunch of people

sitting around trying to recreate the world's literature from memory, you're only ever going to get pale imitations, no matter how many PhDs you have working at it."

"Speaking of which . . . "

Paul groaned again and leaned back in his seat. On days like this, he wanted to dig a hole in the earth, crawl inside, and shovel the dirt on top of himself. That wasn't an option though. He had taken this job, and they paid him well for it. Reasonably well, anyway, though lately it didn't seem like nearly enough.

"What's the problem?" he said, deciding that he'd had enough self-pity for the day. Tackling problems he could actually deal with usually made him feel better, less impotent.

"While you were out, I had a few manuscripts turned in," Alison said, tapping the screen of her tablet. "I skimmed through them, and there are a couple of issues."

"Lay it on me."

"Susie Langley just finished *The Firm* by John Grisham, but I think she may have mixed up the plots of several of his books and combined them into one. However, I'm not familiar enough with his work to know for sure."

Paul shrugged. "From what I remember of his books, people aren't likely to notice, but I'll take a look at it, see if I can untangle the threads."

"Well, that's the least of our worries."

"What do you mean?"

"Jasper Phillips turned in his first draft for *Romeo and Juliet*."

"Jasper is one of our most talented restoration artists. What's wrong with the manuscript?"

"Well, he has Juliet waking up just before Romeo drinks the poison, and they run off together to live happily ever after."

Paul's frown deepened to the point where he thought the corners of his mouth must be hanging off his face. "He actually thinks that's the way the play ended?"

"No, he knows the play was a tragedy, but he said while we were restoring literature we might as well try *improving* it as well."

"What?"

"Oh yes, and he gave me a whole list of other books he thought we could improve. I'll tell you, after perusing his list, his idea of improvement seems to be taking anything with an unhappy ending and giving it a happy one."

"Did Joel have anything to say about it? He's Mr. By-the-Book, pardon the pun."

"You know J.J. They have each other's backs even if one of them is blatantly in the wrong."

"Great. I'll have a talk with Jasper. In the meantime—"

"Only assign him stories where the original already has a happy ending? Way ahead of you."

"You're a godsend, Alison," Paul said, and he meant it. As much as the woman's fastidiousness sometimes annoyed him, he would be lost without her.

"That's why they pay me the medium bucks."

"You really should be doing my job."

Alison laughed, but the sound was perfunctory. "No thanks. I think the stress would be a bit too much."

"Yeah, you and me both."

She stood and headed from the office, pausing at the threshold. "By the way, a FedEx package arrived from Greg Nylon."

"Awesome. What did we get?"

"He shipped us an illustrated edition of *Alice's Adventures in Wonderland* in fairly decent shape. I've already catalogued it, scanned it into the system, and placed the physical copy into the vault."

"Thanks. Don't suppose he included any kind of progress report, did he?"

"Nope, just the book." As she left the office, she called over her shoulder, "I've forwarded you all the manuscripts turned in while you were gone as well as Jasper's list."

Paul pulled his tablet from his satchel and booted up the system to get some work done. Instead of opening the folder for "Restorations", however, he tapped on the one labeled "Acquisitions". The brevity of the files saddened him, but he refused to dwell. At least one more title had been added to it.

He tapped on the file for the Lewis Carroll novel, opening the scanned document. The title page seemed to be missing, but scrolling through the rest of the manuscript, he was happy to see the story itself intact and the text relatively clean and legible. The illustrations were a bit fuzzy, but once the book was transferred into a digital file, these would be removed anyway.

Paul couldn't turn his thoughts away from Greg Nylon. He supervised the Acquisitions Department, and a week and a half ago, he'd gone on what he called a "scavenging mission", tracking down leads on some children's literature he'd been told were on display in a museum in the Upstate of South Carolina. Paul hadn't heard from him since he'd left, and this copy of *Alice's Adventures in Wonderland* was the first evidence he'd seen that Greg's leads had born any fruit.

He placed the tablet on his desk, reached up to the small plastic bulb in his right ear and tapped it twice, opening a line. He enunciated, "Call Greg N." A few beeps followed, and then came the purring ring that seemed to emanate from inside his head.

After four rings, Paul started thinking he was going to get Greg's voicemail, but halfway through the fifth ring, static crackled on the line followed by the roaring *whoosh* of a wind tunnel and the sound of heavy breathing.

"Greg?" Paul said.

At first, there was no response except for the wind and the panting, but then a single strained word. "Willie . . . ?"

Willie. Greg's nickname for Paul, based on the fact that his boss shared the same last name as some archaic singer Greg liked. No one else ever called him that.

"Greg, what are you doing? Running a marathon?"

No answer, but underneath the wind, Paul thought he detected the faint sound of other voices, though he couldn't make out any words. Greg spoke again, but his voice was lost in a burst of static. Paul thought he heard the words "*in danger*", but he couldn't be sure. Before he could respond, the line went dead, just a dull buzzing in his ear.

Frowning, Paul reset the line and tried calling again, but this time, it went straight to voicemail. The next two times, he got the same result.

Tendrils of unease wound around Paul's chest, squeezing tight. He briefly considered contacting the authorities, but the voice of reason spoke up in his head, sounding remarkably like Alison.

Don't be ridiculous. You've known Greg for years, which means you know he does things his own way. He often goes incommunicado for weeks at a time while he's out on scavenging missions, and it wouldn't be the first time he forgot to charge his cell. That's probably all that happened; his cell was dying just as you called. That would explain all the static. He'll be in touch when he's ready, just like always.

All that made sense, of course. Last spring, Greg had disappeared for almost three weeks, finally showing back up at the office with a tan, saying he'd been scouring for books at Myrtle Beach. Paul would probably have been a lot angrier if the man hadn't returned with the complete *Boxcar Children* series.

Trying to put the incident out of his mind, Paul picked up his tablet to get to work going through the file for *The Firm*, but he kept hearing the last two words he thought he'd made out from Greg.

. . . in danger . . .

LATE NIGHT PHONE CALLS

"**C**AN YOU BELIEVE the nerve of that prick?" Jasper said as he paced back and forth at the foot of the bed.

Joel rinsed, spit, then flipped off the bathroom light as he stepped back into the bedroom. "Honey, let it go."

"Let it go? Let it go, you say! You weren't the one dragged into Mr. Nelson's office and lambasted all because you were thinking outside the box."

"We're not paid to think outside the box."

"That's dreck, Joel. We're supposed to be giving the world good literature to read, and that's what I'm trying to do."

"I know, but you can't go and change the endings to books simply because you don't like them."

"Why not? Everything from dish detergent to anti-virus software is constantly releasing 'New and Improved' versions. If I can make it better, why not?"

Joel walked over to his husband and grabbed his shoulders, forcing him to stop pacing. "I think you've got too much pent-up creativity, that's all. If you asked Mr. Nelson, I'm sure he'd grant you some time off to finish *Down by the Waterside*."

Jasper's expression hardened, his eyes squinting

as his lips pulled down into a slight frown. He jerked out of Joel's grasp and stalked across the room. "I'm going to get a snack before bed," he said as he stormed into the hallway, closing the door behind him with a tad too much force.

With a sigh, Joel crawled into bed, grabbing his tablet from the nightstand so he could work on his restoration of *The Sound and the Fury.* He'd only brought up Jasper's novel-in-progress to be encouraging, but he realized now it'd been a mistake.

Joel and Jasper had first met when they were in the postgraduate program at the University of South Carolina—quickly becoming inseparable and earning the collective nickname of J.J.—and even then, Jasper had been dreaming of penning the Great American Novel. A walking cliché, some might say, but his passion had been effusive and infectious and was one of the reasons Joel had fallen in love with the man.

They'd married just after earning their degrees in English Lit, and Jasper had spent the next three years working on *Down by the Waterside.* Even with Joel, he was secretive about the project, preferring not to let anyone read any of it while the manuscript was in progress. Joel wasn't even entirely sure of the plot.

Joel had known plenty of writers at university, most of which had found great joy in the act of writing. Not Jasper. Writing seemed a chore for him, one that left him frustrated and depressed. Joel knew this was because of Jasper's perfectionist nature; he often beat himself up for perceived self-failings which existed solely in his head.

The night of their third anniversary, Jasper had gotten drunk and confessed that all he had to show for these years of work were four pitiful chapters, a total of seventy-five pages. He said he continued going back through these chapters to get them just right, but he always found something worth tweaking, polishing, but still found the prose lacking.

Then the Wipe occurred.

When Joel volunteered for the restoration program, Jasper had eagerly joined him, throwing himself into the work with an abandon that bordered on joyous. Joel suspected his husband was secretly relieved to have this distraction from his own crumbling literary aspirations. It had been months since Jasper had even mentioned the novel.

Then Joel had gone and brought it up when Jasper was already upset. Not exactly his most sensitive move.

He placed the tablet back on the counter and got out of bed. First rule of a successful marriage, according to his mother, was knowing when to admit you were wrong.

Joel started down the hall toward the front of the house, thinking of different ways to apologize beyond a simple "I'm sorry." Tomorrow was Saturday, so perhaps he'd get up early and make a huge breakfast of waffles, pancakes, and sausage and serve Jasper in bed. Of course, there were other things he could do in bed to smooth things over.

As he turned into the dining room, through which one reached the kitchen, his pace faltered. He heard murmuring through the kitchen's swinging door, and he crept up to it on bare feet, moving slowly and carefully so none of the floorboards would creak beneath him. At the door, he paused, leaning his head close.

Jasper was talking all right, his voice low but audible. Presumably on his cell. Joel leaned closer until his ear almost touched the door itself, listening to his husband's side of this whispered conversation.

"No, I already told you, Joel doesn't know a thing. I don't want to bring him in on this because I don't think he'd understand what we want to accomplish. They don't call him Mr. By-the-Book down at the office for nothing, you know. Yes, I'm trying, but that damn Nelson blocks me every step of the way, and the Wyatt bitch backs his every play. I'm telling you, we need them out of the picture if we're ever going to make any progress."

Biting his lip, Joel slowly backed away from the door, practically tiptoeing until he reached the hall, then scurried back to the bedroom. He turned out the light and crawled under the covers, and when Jasper returned a few minutes later and called his name softly, he didn't respond, feigning sleep.

He felt the mattress shift as Jasper crawled in next to him, and within moments, he heard his husband's distinctive rattling snore. Joel opened his eyes and stared into the darkness, his mind whirring. This wasn't the first clandestine phone call he'd accidentally overheard in the past month. Jasper thought he was being sneaky, but he was no secret agent.

At first, Joel had entertained the notion that Jasper was cheating on him, but it quickly became clear this had something to do with work, with Mr. Nelson and Ms. Wyatt. What was this about, though, and who was Jasper talking with? A quick peek at Jasper's tablet and the call history would answer his questions, but Joel felt ashamed at the mere thought of invading Jasper's privacy.

The second rule for a successful marriage, Joel's mother had imparted to him, was never to keep secrets from one another.

Well Mom, Joel thought as he closed his eyes, *that rule has already been broken in this house, so where do we go from here?*

※

As midnight approached, Paul sat up in bed with a book opened on his lap.

Not a digital book on his tablet but an honest-to-goodness print book made from paper and cloth. *Great Expectations* by Charles Dickens. A hardcover with stained yellow pages, a cracked spine, and loose binding. In fact, several pages had fallen out and were stuffed back into place. The book had been in his family for at least five generations, the name of his great-great-grandfather scrawled on the inside cover in faded ink.

Paul had read the novel several times, and usually when he pulled it out of the safe, it wasn't to re-familiarize himself with a story he practically knew by heart—he would have done the restoration himself if that wouldn't have seemed odd; instead he'd assigned it to Joel, who had done an acceptable, albeit clumsy, job. No, he brought out *Great Expectations* so he could feel it in his hands, breathe in the musty aroma, hear the sound of the brittle pages like dried leaves scraping along pavement. A totally immersive sensory experience. Sometimes he entertained the silly notion of licking the book, imagining it would taste of exotic spices.

The only person who knew he had the book was

Greg. At last year's Christmas party, feeling slightly tipsy and forlorn, Paul had mentioned it to the other man, but luckily Greg had proven capable of keeping a secret. Not that Paul was doing anything illegal, but the head of the Southeastern Library withholding a book certainly wouldn't look good and could conceivably lead to a reprimand from the subcommittee.

Paul had considered turning the novel in many times, but if he did, it would become the property of the United States government. It would be scanned and then locked away in the vault with the other print books his team had managed to procure over the years. Then he'd never be able to touch or smell it again, not to mention losing a touchstone to his ancestry.

At the bottom of it all, childish as it was, he simply didn't want to.

Paul read the final line of *Great Expectations*, which never failed to give him chills, and closed the book. He mused how this novel could be used by Jasper Phillips to prove some kind of point since Dickens' original ending had been much more downbeat. The difference, of course, was that the author himself had chosen to alter the ending of the story prior to publication, and the original ending only became known when it was included as a footnote in John Forster's biography *The Life of Charles Dickens*.

Paul raised the book to his face and inhaled deeply. He imagined he could smell not only the history of the physical book but the history of the story itself. That part of the perfume was Dickens' sweat, the scent of the parchment on which he wrote, the ink which soaked into the pages to create the words that'd survived centuries.

At least until the Wipe.

Yet the words did survive, right here in Paul's hands.

He swung his legs out of the bed and walked across the room to the framed print of van Gogh's *The Starry Night*. The painting actually swung out and away from the wall on a hidden hinge to reveal a small wall safe. He pressed his thumb against the safe's scanner, a green light glowing as it read his fingerprint. A minute *click* as the lock disengaged. After sliding the copy of *Great Expectations* into a clear plastic sleeve and sealing it, he placed the book into the safe and closed the steel door.

Just as he swung the painting back into place, his tablet chirped from the foot of the bed, the distinctive tone alerting him to an incoming call. He hurried over, glancing at the screen at the number on the display. He didn't recognize it, but the area code was for the Upstate area. Greg's last known location.

Instead of grabbing his earpiece off the dresser, he simply swiped his finger across the screen to answer the call on speaker.

"Hello."

"Yes, is this Mr. Paul Nelson?"

"It is. To whom am I speaking?"

"My name is Bryant Stevens. I'm the Sheriff in Greer, South Carolina."

Paul's mouth became dry, his palms sweating. He tried speaking but only managed a dry coughing sound. Paul cleared his throat. "Uh, what can I do for you, Sheriff?"

"Are you the employer of a Gregory Nylon?"

A chill spread over every inch of Paul's skin, and he sank down onto the bed. "Yes, I am."

"When was the last time you spoke with Mr. Nylon?"

"Well, I called him just this afternoon."

"You spoke to him? What did he say?"

"Not much actually. We had a bad connection, and the call dropped. I wasn't able to get back in touch with him after that."

"Was there any indication of where he might be?"

"I'm sorry, Sheriff, but what is this about?"

A pause on the other line. "You see, Mr. Nelson, a Honda Furia was reported abandoned at Greer City Park earlier today. I ran the license plate and found it was registered to Gregory Nylon and upon investigation found his wallet and some other personal items inside the car."

"What makes you think the car was abandoned?"

"According to the report filed this afternoon, the car has been parked there for nine days."

Nine days? Paul did some quick calculations and realized this meant the car would have been left at Greer City Park on the same day Greg first arrived in the town, which didn't make any sense.

"Sheriff, my office also received a package from him today, so he can't have been missing for that long."

"That is curious. We ran a check with local motels and did find that a Greg Nylon registered at a Super 8 last Thursday, paying in advance for five days, but no one at the motel ever saw him again after that, and a search of his room turned up no evidence of him staying there at all."

Paul rubbed furiously at his temples, as if he could force all of this information to come together and form a coherent picture, but he had no luck.

"Mr. Nelson," the sheriff said, his voice tinny through the tablet speaker, "I don't know what's going on here, but I'm afraid something may have happened to your employee."

◦◦◦

Alison had fallen asleep on the sofa while watching *Gone Girl* on the TV wall. She loved old films, especially those based on classic literature. However, she recognized these adaptations were dangerous in her current line of work. Earlier in the year, one of the restoration artists had turned in a manuscript for *Frankenstein*, which demonstrated he only had a working knowledge of the early film versions, which varied greatly from the source material.

She'd been musing on this as she drifted off, a half-finished glass of red wine on the coffee table and the bulb for her cell phone still nestled in her ear. The gentle vibrating purr in her ear woke her from a dream of flat-headed monsters with bolts coming out of their necks for no reason.

Stretching languidly, she said aloud, "Mute," silencing the sound on the television. As she sat up, she tapped the ear-bulb once to answer the call. "Hello," she muttered, stifling a yawn.

"Alison, I'm sorry to wake you."

"Paul? What time is it?"

"Half-past midnight. I should have waited until tomorrow, I know, but I have to tell you that I'll be out of the office next week, and I'm going to need you to run things in my absence."

"Is everything okay? Some kind of family emergency?"

"No, it's just . . . well, Greg appears to be missing."

Alison rubbed at her eyes, wiping away the grit her grandmother had always called "sleep dust", wondering if she might have woken from one dream into another. "What do you mean, missing?"

"I don't have all the details. Hell, I don't have *any* details. I'm heading to Greer first thing in the morning, or later this morning to be exact, to meet with the sheriff. I'll contact you as soon as I have more information."

"Greer? Is that the little town with the water tower shaped like a giant peach?"

"No, you're thinking about Gaffney. Greer is between Spartanburg and Greenville."

"Oh," she said. The location of Greer wasn't terribly important, but what else could she say? "How long will you be there?"

"I don't know. It depends on what I can turn up. Sheriff Stevens thinks it'll benefit the investigation if he has someone who knows Greg helping him out."

"Investigation? I'm having trouble wrapping my brain around this."

"You and me both. Again, I'm sorry about waking you. The Library is in your hands; I know you'll handle things fine while I'm gone. If anyone asks, say I came down with the flu. I don't want word about this getting around until we have something more concrete."

"Don't worry, I'll keep it quiet."

"Thanks, Alison. I don't tell you enough, but I couldn't do this job without you."

She found herself speechless. She and Paul sometimes had a contentious relationship, though it was clear they both harbored respect for one another, but such a bald compliment was rare.

"I'll call you when I have news," Paul said. The line went dead.

Alison removed the bulb from her ear and set it down beside her wine glass, which she picked up and brought to her lips. She still felt half-asleep, processing the conversation.

Greg Nylon . . . missing. He was known around the office for disappearing without a word for small stretches of time, his friendship with Paul, as well as his success rate at procuring print books—the only things keeping him from finding himself unemployed. So if Paul was worried, and the authorities in Greer were involved, this must be something other than his usual vanishing act.

This must be serious.

WELCOME TO GREER

PAUL WALKED INTO the police station and stepped up to the counter. A pretty blonde with her hair pulled into a tight bun at the nape of her neck offered him a polite smile. "How may I help you, sir?"

"I'm looking for the sheriff. My name is—"

"Paul Nelson?" said a voice to the left. A tall, lanky man with ebony skin and a bald cranium stood in the doorway of an office behind the counter. No more than thirty, he looked smart in his neatly pressed uniform, gold badge gleaming under the overhead fluorescents.

"Sheriff Stevens, I presume?"

"In the flesh." The man came over to the counter and opened a small door to the right. "Pleased to meet you."

Paul shook the man's hand, noting his firm grip though not aggressively so. "Well, I wish I could say this was a pleasure, but—"

"Of course. Would you like a cup of java?"

Paul was not in the mood for pleasantries or bitter precinct coffee, so he smiled tightly and said, "If it's all the same to you, can I see the car?"

"Sure. Follow me."

Sheriff Stevens led him down a hallway past other offices and a short corridor blocked by a barred door, which Paul assumed led to the holding cells. Stevens talked as they walked.

"We had the car towed in this morning and placed it in our impound lot out back."

"Who reported it, if I can ask?"

"Some folks who live across the street from the park. Noticed the same car there for several days, including overnight, and finally decided to call it in."

"Do they remember seeing him at all?"

"No. We did find a groundskeeper who thought he might recollect seeing someone get out of that car sometime last week, though he wasn't sure of the day, and when we showed him the picture on Mr. Nylon's license, he said he couldn't be sure of that either."

They'd reached a large, metal door at the end of the hall. Stevens pushed down on the crash bar and led Paul out into a cement-paved courtyard, surrounded by a chain-link fence on three sides, razor-wire strung along the top. Half a dozen cars were parked inside the fence, but Paul's gaze zeroed in on Greg's burnt-orange Furia.

Not waiting for the sheriff, Paul hurried over to the car. There was the ding in the driver's side door where Greg had once opened it onto a fence post and the cracked rearview mirror he'd never bothered to replace. Trailing around to the back of the car, Paul saw the familiar bumper sticker: "ALL THE WORLD'S HISTORY CAN BE FOUND IN BOOKS!"

"This is Greg's car, all right," Paul said softly. He'd been hoping it wouldn't be and that this would all prove to be some mistake.

Stevens stood a few feet away, as if he understood Paul needed some space to let this all sink in. Before, it had been theoretical; actually seeing and running his fingers along the car made it real.

Paul placed his hands on the dusty trunk of the car and envisioned Greg's easy smile; the disheveled hair seemed incapable of being tamed. Paul didn't often think in such grammar school terms, but he supposed if he had a best friend, it would be Greg. His devil-may-care attitude was a great counterpoint to Paul's often pathological seriousness. Paul couldn't imagine life without him.

Stop being melodramatic. He's not dead. Sure, this is all strange as hell, but keep in mind he mailed you a book earlier in the week, and you talked to him just yesterday. Sort of.

"You said his wallet was in the car?" Paul asked.

Stevens nodded. "Yes, in the glove compartment, along with the key-fob for the car."

"The key-fob was inside the car?"

"Yes, it was."

"Why would he do that?"

Stevens didn't answer.

Paul opened the driver's side door and was about to climb inside when he paused. "Is this okay?" he asked the sheriff.

"Sure. We already scanned for fingerprints."

"And?"

"Only prints in the vehicle match the ones we found for Mr. Nylon in the federal registry."

"Have you done a search on his account to see if he's spent any money?"

"Of course," Stevens said in the weary tone of someone sick of people assuming he doesn't know how to do his job. "The day he paid for his motel room, he also ran up quite the tab at a local bar and then purchased an assortment of alcohol from a nearby liquor store."

Paul frowned. "That's odd. Greg has never been a big drinker."

"He either decided to give drinking a try or he met someone who had a taste for the sauce. Anyway, since then there has been no movement on his account whatsoever, and the tracking chip in his tablet has been deactivated. It's like he doesn't want to be found."

"Or someone doesn't want him to be found," Paul said as he slid behind the wheel, settling into the leather seat. He didn't know what he possibly hoped to accomplish by this. Not likely he would sit here and discover a clue the cops had overlooked, some fabric fiber or strand of hair that would make sense of everything.

Running his fingers along the dash, then tapping the pink fuzzy dice hanging from the rearview, causing them to sway back and forth like a pendulum, he finally turned his attention back to Stevens. "Where is this park where the car was found?"

"Greer City Park, a few blocks from here."

"I want to go there."

"I'll take you, but first, there's something else I think you should see."

"What's that?"

"Let's head back to my office, and I'll show you."

❦

Stevens' office was a small cube, sparsely decorated. Nothing sat on his desk except for a tablet placed precisely in the center. The walls were bare except for one generic framed print of a sunset, possibly once blazing with color but now faded and somewhat sad. The room contained no personal items. No family photos, children's drawings, no knickknacks or trophies. In fact, if not for Stevens sitting behind the desk, Paul would have sworn the office was unoccupied.

The sheriff opened one of the desk drawers and pulled out a clear plastic bag with a piece of paper inside. This he tossed on the desktop next to the tablet. "This was also found in the glove compartment of the car."

Paul stepped up to the desk and stared down at the paper through the plastic. The title page of *Alice's Adventures in Wonderland*. The paper was yellowed and looked brittle, the left edge ragged from where it had been ripped out of the book. In the top right corner were some squiggly lines drawn in blue ink.

"I don't know what this scribbling is," Stevens said, tapping a finger against the plastic above the blue ink. "Some of it almost looks like letters, but I can't make heads or tails of it. How about you?"

Paul grunted and shook his head, hoping the sheriff couldn't see his blatant lying. He knew exactly what the scribbling was. Cursive handwriting, a skill that had stopped being taught in schools long before even the print book went out of fashion. These days the only people who learned cursive were history majors, who needed to read historical documents.

Paul and Greg had both been history majors in college.

Paul could read the words scrawled on the page

easily, and he also recognized it as Greg's handwriting. The message read:

Follow Alice down the rabbit hole, and she'll show you the way to me.

THE INSCRIPTION

I CAN'T BELIEVE *I'm doing this*, Alison thought as she pulled her car into the lot. Like most government facilities, the Library was closed on weekends and all major holidays, yet here she was on a Saturday afternoon going into the office.

All on some strange errand for Paul, who hadn't even bothered to explain the significance of this off-hours mission.

Not that she'd been in the middle of anything major when Paul had called, just out back pulling weeds from her small vegetable garden.

"Alison, it's Paul. I need to ask you some questions about the book Greg sent us."

"Paul, is everything okay? Have you found out anything about him?"

"No, nothing yet, but I need to know about the book."

"Alice's Adventures in Wonderland?"

"That's the one. You said there was no note or anything with the book. Are you sure there was nothing else?"

"Positive. Nothing but the book."

"What about the actual packaging, any writing on that?"

"Just the address. Paul, what is this about?"

"I don't want to get into it right now because it may be nothing. Was there any kind of message that came along with the book?"

"No. The only writing other than the address was an inscription on the inside front cover."

"An inscription! Do you remember what it said?"

"I couldn't read it. It was written in cursive script."

"I'm going to need you to take a picture of that inscription and message it to me."

"Why?"

"Please don't ask questions. Just trust that it's important."

"Okay, first thing Monday—"

"No, now. I need you to go to the Library right now."

"Paul, what exactly is going on?"

"I promise as soon as I figure it out, I'll let you in on whatever this is. Until then, please don't ask any more questions because I simply don't have any answers."

"Just tell me you're okay."

"I'm okay, Alison, but I need to see that inscription."

And so here she was, walking across the deserted parking lot, listening to her heels clicking hollowly on the pavement. She could have refused Paul's request, at least until he provided her with some kind of explanation, but the thought had never seriously crossed her mind. Alison had a sense of duty to her job as strong as the responsibility parents felt toward their children, and though she couldn't begin to fathom what would prompt Paul to send her on this errand, she did not doubt his reasons.

For all their head-butting, Alison respected Paul more than anyone she'd ever met. She knew his position as head of the Library often frustrated him, but that was precisely what made him perfect for the job. He harbored genuine passion for the work and would not sit idly by as the government tried to shut down Acquisitions in favor of Restoration. Ultimately, he may not be able to stop that tide from rolling in, but Alison knew he wouldn't go down without a fight.

At the door, she placed her right palm on the scanner. Two seconds later, she heard the *click* as the door unlocked and the alarm deactivated. Stepping inside, she noted the utter quiet. Normally, the large open space of the main room was full of people and their accompanying noise. True to the moniker the place had, the noise was always of the hushed variety—murmured conversations between cubicles, the soft tapping of fingers pecking and swiping at touchscreens, the creaking of chairs and rustling of clothes. The normal hum of an office environment. Something that fades into the background on a daily basis and you don't even notice.

Until it's gone.

She walked through the utter silence, feeling as if she were on the set of one of those popular post-apocalyptic movies. At the back, she turned left, going past the offices to the large metal door of the vault. Here Alison placed her palm against another scanner while leaning forward and saying her name clearly and loudly. The vault lock disengaged with a resounding *clunk*.

A staircase leading down to the building's basement waited on the other side of the door. Alison descended quickly, going through a second door at the base of the stairs into the chilled air of the vault. The entire open space was filled with bookshelves, and whenever Alison came down here, she liked to imagine all the shelves weighed down by volumes crammed side by side, like in the old photographs she'd seen of ancient libraries. However, those were what dreams and memory were made of. Not even half the shelves in the vault were filled. The glaring overhead fluorescents illuminated a fairly depressing scene.

Each book housed in the vault was sealed in plastic with a cataloguing label containing title and author information. Alison went straight to where she'd placed the book earlier in the day and pulled it down, removing it from the plastic sleeve. She took a seat at an old school desk in the nearest corner and opened the book to the front inside cover.

The inscription stood there as she remembered it. Shaky, illegible scrawling that may as well have been in another language for all she knew. She swiped a finger across her tablet to bring up the home screen and tapped the camera icon. Positioning the tablet just above the book, she took a shot and quickly sent it as a message to Paul's number.

$\sim\!\!\downarrow\!\!\sim$

Paul sat on the edge of the bed in his motel room. The Super 8, the same motel where Greg had rented a room ten days earlier. It could even be the same room.

None of this made any sense, and solving a puzzle that appeared to have no solution left Paul with a throbbing headache. He stood and began pacing the cramped room, stopping by the window looking out on the parking lot and down to Wade Hampton Boulevard. The lights in the room were off, but the murky afternoon glow filtered through the window in bars of dust.

His thoughts kept turning to the message written on the crumpled title page of the book. *Follow Alice down the rabbit hole, and she'll show you the way to me.* Cryptic poetry. What was the point of that? Why not leave a straightforward message? For that matter, why leave a message in this way at all? Why not just call or text?

He paced some more, settling on the foot of the bed, contemplated turning on the TV wall while he waited to hear back from Alison, but then dismissed the idea. His head was noisy enough without the added empty chatter from the idiot box.

Greg had always been a bit of a jokester, but Paul couldn't believe this was a game. It was too elaborate. The motel room he never stayed in, the car being abandoned since the day he arrived in town, the broken up phone call with voices in the background. All he had before him were a bunch of pieces that didn't seem to fit together into a cohesive whole.

Another question he had to ask of himself was why he hadn't told Sheriff Stevens he was able to read Greg's message. For some reason, he had felt the need to hold that information back. Was it a crime, impeding an investigation? Should he contact the officer now and come clean, or would his confession merely make matters worse?

Paul's tablet chirped with an incoming message. He snatched up the device and quickly opened the attached photo. He stared at the inscription for a moment. Definitely Greg's handwriting again, two sentences. The first sentence didn't make much sense, but it was the second sentence that captured Paul's attention.

Dearest Willie, meet me at the Greer Theater, and purchase tickets for the matinee of Creature from the Black Lagoon. Afterwards, I'll show you the way to Book Haven!

Article from **The Online Encyclopedia of Modern Myths and Urban Legends:**

The story of Book Haven is a persistent urban legend that arose shortly after the event most have come to know as *The Wipe*, an insidious computer virus that eradicated all digital copies of the world's literature.

According to the legend, somewhere in the United States is a secret underground library that houses thousands to millions (the number varies depending on the account) of antique paper books. If such a library truly existed, the value in today's market would be nearly incalculable.

The lure of such a lucrative payday has led many over the years to "hunt" for Book Haven. The most famous case was vlogger *Gerald Rivers*. Rivers chronicled his six-month search online, convinced he was on the right track based on a statistical analysis of the areas of the country where the most antique books had been located by both the various branches of the *Institute for Acquisition and Restoration of Literature* as well as the independent contractors known as *"Book Hounds."* Rivers did not concentrate his search in these areas, however, but instead found the location with the least antique books acquired, his theory being that all the books in this area were being hoarded for Book Haven. He deduced that the library must exist somewhere in the Great Plains area of Montana. Rivers scoured the state, interviewing hundreds of people, but ultimately came up empty-handed. Instead of admitting he may have been wrong, he instead deduced Book Haven had been moved once whoever maintained the library realized he was on to them.

Another well-known event related to Book Haven was the *Haven Hoax*, in which a group of individuals in the hamlet of Haven, New York, announced they were the keepers of the secret library and had decided to share the books with the world, orchestrating a public auction for hundreds of volumes. However, an independent government appraisal revealed the books to be forgeries. Those responsible were charged with fraud and fined an undisclosed sum.

Despite all the searching, no

concrete or definitive evidence has ever been found to corroborate the existence of Book Haven. In fact, the story varies among geographic regions. Like most urban legends, everyone seems to think Book Haven is somewhere in their part of the country and that a friend of a friend of a friend has firsthand knowledge of it. Similar stories have also been noted in other countries such as France and Italy.

Most experts agree this particular legend has no basis in reality and the mythic Book Haven unfortunately does not exist . . .

GATHERING THE TROOPS

JASPER GRIPPED THE steering wheel as if he wanted to snap it in half. "I don't understand why I'm on this trip?" he said through clenched teeth.

In the passenger's seat, Joel stared out the window and watched the scenery blurring by. He considered asking his husband to slow down as they were traveling upwards of twenty miles per hour over the posted speed limit, but considering Jasper's current mood, such a suggestion would only lead to an argument.

Turning his gaze to his husband, Joel said, "At least we're together. Is that so bad?"

Jasper sighed. "I didn't mean it like that. With Paul and Alison both out of the office, I should be running the place, not sent on some pointless mission like an errand boy. I mean, they left that incompetent Susie Langley in charge. We'll be lucky if she doesn't burn the place down while we're gone."

"That's not fair. Susie happens to have a PhD in Early American Lit."

"Please, the woman keeps stuffed animals on her desk. The only reason Alison asked both of us to come to Greer is because she's intimidated by me and doesn't want me showing her up while she's with Paul.

I'm probably the most valuable asset they have at the Library, and they are totally wasting me on this wild goose chase."

"Greg is missing, so I for one am happy to do anything I can to help find him."

"He's not missing. This whole thing is just some elaborate prank. I mean, Book Haven? Everybody knows that isn't real. No, Greg is just playing some stupid game, and Paul and Alison are falling for it and dragging us along with them."

"I know Greg can be a little . . . unorthodox at times, but I seriously doubt he'd have us waste all this time and resources for a prank. Besides, did he somehow get the sheriff and half the city of Greer to go along with him?"

With a snort, Jasper took his eyes off the road long enough to cast a sidelong glance at his husband. "Don't tell me that you believe in the fairytale of Book Haven?"

"No, but something odd is going on, and Greg seems to have gotten himself caught in the middle of it. I think we owe it to him to figure this out."

"It's not like we're even friends with him. Hell, I've probably spoken two words to him in the last year, if that."

"He's still a colleague, and he might be in trouble."

Jasper glanced at Joel again, but this time, a smile curled the edges of his lips. "I really did marry a Good Samaritan, didn't I?"

Joel laughed. It was a running joke, Jasper often calling him either Good Samaritan or Boy Scout. It was definitely better than Mr. By-the-Book. "Well, I have to be a Good Samaritan to balance out your Grinch tendencies."

"I guess that's why we work so well together."

"You're yin to my yang."

Jasper took one hand off the wheel to squeeze Joel's knee. "Okay, I promise no more bitching . . . at least until we get to Greer."

"Deal," Joel said and took his husband's hand. The exchange felt like something to treasure, a rare moment of light-hearted fun that reminded Joel of the early days of their relationship, when they both found each other's differences fascinating instead of irritating and divisive. Joel could almost forget the secret late-night phone calls and the sense of invisible walls between them.

"Damn it," Jasper said, removing his hand and placing it back on the wheel in its previous death grip.

"What's wrong?"

"Battery light just came on."

Before his brain had time to curb his mouth, Joel said, "I told you before we left we needed to charge it."

Jasper sighed heavily and throttled the steering wheel even tighter.

"That wasn't an 'I told you so'," Joel was quick to add, not wanting to damage the fragile peace which had settled in the car. "I could have done it myself, but I didn't."

Glancing down at the GPS display on the console, Jasper said, "There's a charging station about a mile up the road. I'm sure we can make it there."

Joel also glanced at the display. "There's a diner next to the station. Maybe we can grab an early lunch."

"I'm not hungry," Jasper said. "Feel free to get something, though. I have some phone calls to make."

—\|/—

Alison had been in her motel room at the Super 8 only five minutes when a knock came at the door. She opened it to find Paul standing out in the breezeway.

"That was fast," she said. "I was just getting settled in, hadn't even had a chance to give you a call."

"I'm two doors down, saw you pulling in, thought I'd come on by."

She stepped back to allow Paul to enter. "Come on in; make yourself at home."

Her suitcase sat open on the bed, two of the drawers in the bureau pulled out. Paul wandered to the far corner of the room, where a small, round table was placed like an afterthought. He took a seat in one of the two plastic chairs.

"So when is J.J. arriving?"

"They're about an hour behind me. I wanted to come ahead of them so you and I would have time to talk."

Paul nodded and leaned forward, arms folded on the tabletop. "Okay, so let's talk."

Alison closed the door and sat across from her boss. She formulated her words carefully before allowing them to leave her lips. She settled on a question. "Have you still not told the sheriff about the messages?"

Paul shook his head.

"Any particular reason why not?"

"Greg meant those messages for me, and I don't want to bring in the authorities until I get a better sense of what he's gotten himself into."

"You don't . . . I mean, you're not entertaining the idea that . . . "

"That Book Haven might be more than just a myth?" Paul said, smiling. "I've never put much stock in the story. Just childish wishful thinking as far as I'm concerned. I know Greg felt the same. I believe he called the very notion dreck on more than one occasion. Yet that is definitely his handwriting, so there has to be a reason he would say Book Haven is real."

"From what you've told me of his messages, he seems to be talking in riddles. He may not have intended for the Book Haven reference to be taken literally."

"I've considered as much. It's possible he's telling me he's located a stash of antique books, and maybe he wants to keep the information from a group of Book Hounds or something."

"Still, why disappear like this and send you cryptic messages? It seems a bit extreme. Surely there would be an easier way to get the information to you, don't you think?"

Paul threw up his hands. "The only person who could possibly make sense of this for us is Greg, which is why we need to find him."

"Okay then," Alison said, slipping into her standard proficiency mode, which made her great at her job though not the most popular person with her co-workers. "So what about this Greer Theater? Is it a real place?"

"I did a little research, and it turns out there was a Greer Theater here a long time ago, but it closed down sometime in the twentieth century. The building, however, still exists. It has housed a lot of different businesses over the years but is currently unoccupied.

I managed to get in touch with the current owner and have arranged for him to give us a little tour later this afternoon."

"Has anyone else been in touch with him about the building recently?"

"I asked, but he said no one has been in the building in years, including himself. He has actually considered having it torn down and selling the land."

"Hmm, seems an odd place to arrange a meeting."

"Unless he planted another message there for me, but then again, he would have had to have broken into the building to leave it."

"Paul, I'm going to be honest with you; none of this adds up to anything I can understand, and it worries me."

"I know, but I can't just let this go. I have a friend and a colleague on the line here. I thought if I could get some more brains working on this, maybe we could get to the bottom of the mystery."

Alison reached out, intending to place her hand over Paul's, but she paused and let her hand drop to the tabletop. She respected Paul, and her heart hurt to see him this concerned, but it would be inappropriate to assume such a familiarity with her boss. "I'm here to help in any way I can."

"I appreciate that."

"What time is the tour of the old Greer Theater?"

"Two. I figure once J.J. gets here, we can all have lunch before heading over."

"Sounds good."

"I'll leave you to your unpacking." Paul stood and headed for the door. He glanced back at her. "I really am grateful for your help, Alison."

"Anytime."

After Paul left, Alison returned to her suitcase and began stowing away the clothes she'd brought. Enough for three days. If their search for Greg lasted longer, she'd have to find a laundromat somewhere in this town.

Of course, if their search lasted longer than three days, she may have to have a serious conversation with Paul. She didn't know Greg as well as Paul did, but this bizarre scavenger hunt seemed almost silly, and she couldn't help feeling that Paul was making a mistake by going along with it.

On the other hand, it would mean she was making a mistake by being here.

"Three days," she said to herself as she refolded a blouse before placing it in one of the bureau drawers. "I'll give it three days, and if we haven't come up with anything concrete by then, I'll put my foot down and insist Paul turn over the information about the messages to the sheriff and let them deal with it."

THE GREER THEATER

THE TWO STORY BUILDING that once housed the Greer Theater sat on Main Street a few blocks from the police station. The bricks were a dispirited gray, the color of depression, faded and flaking like a leper sloughing off skin. In the front, facing the street, was a large, plate-glass window with a lightning-bolt crack running through it at a diagonal angle.

Paul and his crew parked at a drug store across the street. The owner of the building, an older gentleman named Becker, stood out front by the window and greeted them enthusiastically.

"Mr. Nelson? Such a pleasure to meet you, Mr. Nelson!" Becker grabbed Paul's hand and pumped it like he would be able to draw water from an old-time well.

Paul grimaced, passed it off as a smile, and freed his hand from the vise-like grip. "I really appreciate you meeting us here, Mr. Becker. I'm sure it must be an inconvenience to you."

"Not at all, not at all. Happy to do it for you fine folks. I couldn't believe it when you told me the government was considering opening a Library facility right here in Greer."

"A Library in Greer?" Jasper said.

Paul winced. He'd neglected to tell Alison and J.J. that he'd finagled this tour by insinuating the government was interested in the building as a possible Library location. "Yes, well, of course Greer is just one of the sites we are considering," he said, cutting a glance at Jasper, whom he hoped would keep quiet and go along with the ruse.

Becker pulled a keycard from his pocket and motioned toward a recessed doorway on the building's left side. "Well, let's get the show on the road. The building needs a little work, but I think you'll see it would be a great space for offices."

As they walked up the two steps to the doorway, Joel said, "Hey, is that a ticket booth?"

A window was located to the right with a small opening at the bottom, the glass smudged and scratched, making it nearly impossible to see through. Becker glanced toward it. "Yes, this building originated as a theater, though the inside has been sufficiently renovated so you'd never be able to tell. When I ran my secondhand shop out of here, I placed an antique mannequin in a vintage usher's uniform in the booth. Customers seemed to get a real kick out of it."

With a swipe of the keycard, Becker opened the door and ushered the group inside. They found themselves in a short entry hall; an open doorway to the right led into the booth. Paul looked at Alison and lifted his chin slightly in that direction. Picking up on his cue, she said, "We might be able to knock out this wall and make this into a lobby of sorts." She stepped into the booth.

"Exactly how long has it been since the building was inspected for structural issues?" Paul asked, walking up to Becker, hoping to distract him as Alison did a thorough search of the booth. With the clue having mentioned buying a ticket, the booth seemed the most likely place to find some message from Greg. He could have slipped it through the opening in the window without even needing to get inside the building.

The booth being so small, Alison emerged within a minute. Becker answered Paul's question about inspections, but Paul wasn't really listening. He merely nodded, and once the other man stopped talking, he turned to Alison and asked, "Everything look good?"

Alison held out her hands. "Some dust and cobwebs, but other than that, nothing of note."

"Yes, I do apologize for the mess, but if you are serious about purchasing the building, I'll have it all cleaned at no expense to you."

Paul nodded again, thinking, *So no clue in the ticket booth. There has to be something somewhere in this building.*

The tour continued. The bulk of the first floor was one big open space, an area that had once been the store. Glass counters and shelving units still filled the space but for the most part were empty. A few items remained: one of those old notebook computers, a globe with South America peeling off, a manual vacuum, and a set of Encyclopedias stacked into a tower. This last feature sent Paul's heart trip-hammering in his chest; he'd have to talk to Becker later about purchasing the set if he could get the Subcommittee to approve the cost.

A variety of smaller rooms opened off the far end of the open area; these may have once been used as offices or possibly for storage. All they contained now were rodent droppings and dead bugs. Paul felt his frustration building, and he found himself looking for cursive messages scrawled in the dust.

When they reached the stairwell at the back of the building, Paul asked, "What's on the second floor?"

Becker hesitated, and his skin flushed. He stammered before getting his words out. "I don't think going upstairs would be such a good idea. The building isn't condemned or anything, but some of the wood up there is rotted. I'm not saying you would fall through, but until I can get those inspections, I wouldn't want to risk it. I hope this won't negatively influence your decision."

"I'll be extra careful where I step," Paul said, suddenly positive that the second floor was where he would find whatever it was he was meant to find.

"I really wouldn't be comfortable if anything did happen. I could be held liable. I'm sure you understand—"

"Excuse me," Alison broke in. "I was wondering if there are any bathroom facilities on this floor?"

Becker smiled, seemingly grateful to have a change of subject, and turned to her. "Oh yes, I neglected to show you the restroom. Come with me."

Alison took Becker's elbow, like a proper lady, and headed back toward the front of the store with J.J. in tow. Paul followed a few steps and then stopped. Alison cast a quick glance over her shoulder, and he mouthed a silent "thank you" before he backtracked to the stairs.

⌇

The second floor was another big open area. He could tell by the difference in color and size that half of the boards were not original to the building though.

This was the balcony, he thought. *When this place was a theater, this was the balcony.*

A half dozen metal desks sat throughout as well as twice the number of moldering boxes with the flaps duct-taped closed. He quickly moved from desk to desk, gritting his teeth at every squeak of the floorboards beneath him. Despite being in a hurry, he tested each step before putting down his full weight.

All the desk drawers were empty except for the occasional pen or bent paperclip. He didn't have time to go through all the boxes, but he checked the duct-tape to see if any of it looked fresh. No luck, the tape was all dirty and frayed and had been applied sometime in the past.

A creaking behind him made Paul spin around, expecting to find Becker standing there, wearing an accusing look. Paul was already planning his apology when he realized it was only Joel, his tablet clutched to his chest.

"What are you doing up here?" Paul asked, walking over to the young man.

"Alison has Becker talking about the building's plumbing, but I came up here to tell you that I think we may be barking up the wrong tree."

"What do you mean?"

Joel held out his tablet. "I've been doing a little additional research into the Greer Theater."

"Please don't tell me I got the wrong building."

"No, this was the Greer Theater, but the ticket booth we saw downstairs is not the original one. When the theater first opened, the ticket booth was a separate structure that jutted out onto the sidewalk."

"What happened to it? Was it torn down?"

"No, actually it was preserved."

"Where?"

"The Greer Heritage Museum."

BUYING A TICKET

THE GREER HERITAGE Museum was also located on Main Street, right next to the police station. Paul briefly wondered if there might be some hidden meaning to all these places being so close together, but with a town as small as Greer, the proximity wasn't actually all that surprising.

A set of stone steps led up to the brick façade, one of the double doors propped open, inviting them inside. The museum consisted of one story with a large open area stretching to the back of the building, a replica of an antique gas-powered car in the middle of the space, and several smaller rooms opening off to the left. From an office to the right stepped an older woman in a pink blouse and red skirt, her white hair coiffed into a cloud atop her head. She wore a nametag which read Patty Davis.

"Welcome to the Greer Heritage Museum," she said with the desperate enthusiasm of someone who hadn't had many visitors lately. "Would you all like the tour?"

Paul nodded. "Is there a fee?"

"Fifteen dollars per person," Patty said, her face scrunched up apologetically. "The museum used to be free to the public, but then the city cut our funding, so we had to start charging."

"It's not a problem. I'll pay for the lot of us."

Patty showed him to a small kiosk with a built-in tablet. Paul typed in his name then pressed his thumb on the scanner, sixty dollars instantly being debited from his bank account. Alison stepped up next to him and said, "What is that?"

Both Paul and Patty followed Alison's gaze and finger. "What are you pointing at dear?" Patty asked.

Just past the automobile, an old-time ticket booth stood against the wall, corrugated silver top and bottom, with glass connecting them. Through the glass, Paul could see a framed movie poster for *Creature from the Black Lagoon* hanging on the wall.

The four librarians hurried across the space to the ticket booth. "Oh, this is an interesting item," Patty said, following along behind them. "This once sat outside a movie theater just a couple of blocks for here. In case you aren't familiar with the term, a movie theater was a place people used to gather in large groups to watch films before home theater systems pretty much put them all out of business."

"I've heard of such things," Jasper said, reaching out to touch to the small opening at the bottom of the glass.

Patty reached out and grabbed the man's wrist. "No touching the displays."

Paul could see several old movie tickets spread out on the counter inside the booth, ten cents a show. He didn't know if these tickets were authentic or replicas—probably the latter, otherwise he felt sure they'd be wrapped in plastic for preservation purposes—but he had to get a closer look at them.

Just like in the old theater building, Alison came to his rescue.

"Excuse me," she said to Patty, "but what are those boxy things with the screens through that doorway there?"

"Oh, those are old desktop computers. We have a refurbished one if you want to see how they worked."

"Please."

Patty led Alison through a door into one of the other rooms, and Paul turned back to the booth and stuck his hand through the opening at the bottom of the glass. Joel and Jasper crowded behind to block him from view should Patty glance back their way. He riffled through the tickets but didn't find any new clues.

"Is anything written on the backs?" Joel asked.

Through the open doorway, Paul heard Alison's voice. "This is amazing. Why were these storage disks called *floppies*?"

Atta girl! Keep her talking til I'm done.

Paul began flipping over the tickets and on the back of the third one found Greg's distinctive scrawl. Quickly pocketing the ticket, he fanned the remaining tickets to get them in the same positioning as they were before he had disturbed them. Or as close as possible. He put his hands behind his back and turned around just as Alison and Patty came back through the doorway.

"Fascinating," Alison said as they rejoined the group. "The graphics were so crude."

Patty nodded. "But a step up from the typewriter. I'd imagine a hundred years from now, our tablets will look fairly prehistoric."

"That's true."

"You have a lovely museum here," Paul said,

hoping he didn't have guilt stamped on his face. When he was a boy, his mother always told him his expression gave him away whenever he'd done something wrong, but Patty Davis wasn't his mother, and he was no longer a boy.

"Why thank you. In the front room, we have a wonderful exhibit that details the changes the city of Greer has undergone over the years through photographs and artifacts, some items dating back to the late 1800s when Greer was founded."

"I don't think we'll have time for—" Jasper started.

"We'd love to. Sounds quite interesting," Paul spoke over him.

They all started back toward the front of the building, Paul ignoring Jasper's glare. It wasn't like Paul wanted to get the most out of the 60 bucks he'd spent on admission, but he figured it would seem suspicious to come into the museum and not take the whole tour.

Suspicious to whom?

Paul wasn't sure, still had no idea what Greg had gotten mixed up in, but he figured the best bet would be to play it safe and not let anyone outside his small group know what they were really doing here.

─✦─

As the foursome exited the museum and walked down the steps to the sidewalk, a voice to their left said, "Mr. Nelson?"

Paul turned, recognizing the voice even before he spotted Sheriff Stevens standing in front of the police station.

"Sheriff, I was just coming to see you," Paul lied as

he walked over to the officer. "I know you said you'd call, but I wanted to check and see if there had been any progress in the investigation."

"I'm afraid we've hit a brick wall unless you've received further information that might be helpful."

"Sorry, I wish I had."

Stevens looked past Paul at the three standing behind him. "Who are your friends?"

"You'll have to forgive my lapse of manners. These are my colleagues. Alison Wyatt and Jasper and Joel Phillips. Guys, this is Sheriff Stevens."

An exchange of pleasantries and then Stevens said, "Had to bring in reinforcements, did you?"

"Well, we do have one of our own missing. What's that old saying? Strength in numbers."

Stevens' gaze flickered toward the museum. "Decided to take in a little local history, I see."

"I figured a local museum would be the first place Greg would go as Head of Acquisitions, so I thought it might be a good idea to ask around," Paul said, realizing only as he said it what a good idea that would have been. However, he'd been so intent on finding Greg's next clue and getting out of there, he hadn't even thought to show Patty the man's photo or ask her any questions.

Stevens nodded. "I thought of that, so I talked with all the staff and even reviewed their surveillance footage, but it doesn't appear he ever went to the museum."

Paul frowned but then forced his face to relax in a blank expression. If Greg had never been in the museum, how had the clue been planted there? Had he come in disguise, or was someone else working with him? Mystery novels had taught Paul that clues typically unraveled a puzzle, but each new clue from Greg only complicated this conundrum, obscuring the path to the truth.

"How long you folks going to be sticking around town?" Stevens asked, looking past Paul toward the other three.

"Not much longer. We have a lot of work piling up back in Columbia," Jasper said.

"I see," Stevens said, turning his eyes back to Paul. "I think the two of us should talk again before you head home."

"Absolutely. I'll call you and set something up."

The two shook hands before Paul and his crew walked down the street, back toward the parking lot where they'd left their vehicle. Glancing over his shoulder, Paul saw Stevens making his way up the steps toward the museum. If he questioned Patty, he'd find out that Paul hadn't actually inquired about Greg at all, which might lead the sheriff to wonder just what the Librarians had really been doing in the museum.

"Are you sure we shouldn't tell the sheriff the truth?" Joel asked, stepping up next to Paul. "Maybe he could help us."

"Maybe, but I'm not sure we can trust him yet."

Jasper snorted. "You're starting to sound a little paranoid. Do you also believe the government is hiding evidence of little green aliens?"

Paul, not normally a man prone to fits of temper or violence, found himself struggling against the sudden desire to whirl around and punch Jasper in the face. He took a few deep breaths to calm himself before saying, "Greg is missing. This is a serious matter."

"It's a waste of time is what it is. We're bureaucrats, not investigators. Leave the police work to the police; we should be back at the Library doing our jobs."

"Speaking of which," Alison said, jumping in before Paul could unleash. "When we get back to the motel, we need to check in at the Library. Jasper, would you mind handling that?"

"Absolutely. I'll make sure everything's under control."

Paul glanced back to see Jasper preening, momentarily irritated with Alison, but then he realized what she was doing—giving him a task that had the illusion of authority to placate him. Smart.

Only once they were back inside the car did Paul pull out the ticket, flipping it over to read Greg's latest message.

Willie, take in the mountain view with Henry Lincoln, and perhaps you'll get a glimpse of the road to Book Haven.

GOING ROGUE

THE FOUR OF them gathered in J.J.'s room. Jasper had called Paul and Alison over about half an hour after they had all returned to the motel.

"So," Paul said, leaning against the wall by the door, "what's the word back at the office?"

Jasper stood in the middle of the room, shoulders squared and chest puffed out, his very posture making the clear statement, *This is* MY *meeting, and I'm in charge here.* Paul thought if the man were a peacock, he would be displaying his colors to impress and intimidate. He paused for dramatic effect, looking at each of them in turn. "Well, it would seem that Senator Kelley has been quite frantic to get in touch with Mr. Nelson."

Paul grimaced. Kelley had been leaving messages all day, and Paul had simply ignored them. Perhaps not the most professional behavior, but he felt justified considering how many calls he'd made to the senator that had gone unanswered.

"I'll call him this evening," Paul said.

Jasper smiled, but it wasn't pleasant. "No need. I took the liberty of getting in touch with him myself."

Paul squeezed his hands into tight fists, his fingernails digging into the flesh of his palms. He had once thought very highly of Jasper, admiring the man's thoroughness and professionalism, but it was clear now that Jasper saw Greg's disappearance as an opportunity for a power grab. A power grab he'd probably been planning for quite a while.

Before Paul could say anything nasty, Alison jumped in. She always seemed to know when to save him from himself. "What did Senator Kelley have to say?"

"He was a bit surprised to find out that Mr. Nelson was still in Greer and even more surprised to find that he had ordered the three of us to join him."

"I didn't *order* anyone," Paul growled. "If you hadn't wanted to come, all you had to do was say so."

Jasper ignored him and went on. "He made it very clear that since this was an unsanctioned excursion, none of us would be paid for our time, and our expenses incurred would not be reimbursed."

"Hell, I'll pay you guys out of my own pocket if that's what you're worried about," Paul said, pushing off the wall. "I'll call him tonight and get all this straightened out."

"No need. You can talk to him tomorrow morning."

"What do you mean? The senator is coming here?"

"No, we're going back to Columbia. He has instructed us to head home tonight. He wants to see us in the office in the morning at 8 sharp."

Paul stood very still, and silence filled the room like a fifth presence, tangible and tense. Finally, he took a deep breath and said, "Okay, fine."

Alison started toward him, said, "Paul, just—", then stopped abruptly. She'd clearly expected him to argue, and his acquiescence surprised her.

Jasper seemed surprised as well, but he recovered quickly. "So it's settled. Let's get packed up, and we can be on the road in half an hour."

Paul nodded. "I guess I don't have much choice in the matter. I'll go get my stuff together."

"This really is for the best," Jasper said, trying and failing to exude a magnanimous air.

Paul said nothing, just opened the door and stepped outside.

—⁂—

Alison followed Paul out onto the breezeway and fell into step next to him. "Paul, I know you're disappointed, but I agree with Jasper that this is for the best. The authorities will continue searching for Greg."

Paul didn't look at her, just stared straight ahead. "The authorities don't have all the information."

"Yes, which is why I think we should turn over the clues to Sheriff Stevens. He may be able to—"

Alison's words cut off, and her pace faltered as she realized they'd passed the door to Paul's room. He continued ahead of her, veering off into the parking lot.

"Paul, where are you going?" she said, hurrying to catch up.

He reached his car then turned back. "I'm going to visit a graveyard."

"What are you talking about?"

"The last clue wasn't difficult to figure out. A quick search for the name Henry Lincoln revealed that he was a writer of detective novels in the mid-21st Century, lived out his life right here in Greer, SC. Guess where he was buried when he died?"

Alison shook her head helplessly.

"The Mountain View Cemetery. That's where the next clue will be."

"We're supposed to be leaving tonight," she said, glancing back toward J.J.'s room.

"You're free to go back to Columbia if you want. I'm going to find Greg."

"Don't you see how crazy this all is?"

Paul stepped toward her, grabbing her lightly by the forearms. His eyes burned with an intensity that frightened her. "What if it's real, Alison?"

"What if what's real?"

"Book Haven! What if the stories about it aren't dreck? What if there's substance to the myth?"

Alison gently removed one of his hands from her arm and squeezed it. "You can't be serious."

"Just think about it. We're scrambling with no budget to try to piece together the world's literature while offering up these pale imitations, but what if there is a place full of antique books, a treasure trove of story? It'd be like striking oil!"

"Striking oil? You're not making any sense."

Paul steadied himself, taking deep breaths and smoothing out the wrinkles in his shirt as if symbolically smoothing out his nerves. "I sound crazy, I know, and maybe it is mad to even entertain the idea of Book Haven's existence. But I've devoted my entire life to books, and I would never be able to live with myself if I left Greer without exhausting every avenue. I understand if you can't go along; I'll likely be fired for insubordination. All I ask is that you let me get out of here before telling J.J."

Alison held out her hand. "Give me your key-fob."

"Please, I'm begging you, let me go."

"You're too worked up to be behind the wheel. I'll drive; you can navigate."

―⁘―

Joel stood a short distance down the breezeway, half-hidden behind one of the columns. He hadn't been able to catch every word of the conversation between Paul and Alison, but he'd heard enough to get the gist. He watched them climb into Paul's car and drive away before he returned to his and Jasper's room.

Across the room, the bathroom door was closed, and he could hear the shower still running, the echo of water beating on tile. Just after Paul and Alison had walked out, Jasper announced he wanted to have a quick rinse before they got on the road and locked himself in the restroom. Joel couldn't help but notice he took his tablet with him.

Creeping up to the bathroom door, he placed his ear against the wood and didn't think he imagined the soft rhythm of fingers tapping the touchscreen.

With a weary sigh, Joel walked to the bed and sat heavily on the lumpy mattress. Jasper's secretiveness was becoming an increasing problem, as was his ambition to run the Library. Joel had tried talking to his husband about this, but Jasper had become more closed-off than usual lately.

What right do I have to be angry about Jasper's secrets when I'm carrying secrets of my own?

Joel reached up and tapped his earbud, resigning himself to making a call he'd been putting off for weeks.

MOUNTAIN VIEW

THE MOUNTAIN VIEW CEMETERY was located in the center of a residential neighborhood several blocks from the downtown area. No fence or gate barred the entrance. One simply drove down a quiet, shady street lined with small but neat wood-framed houses and then came upon the graveyard as if finding an oasis in the midst of a vast desert. Except the opposite of that scenario. Instead of life in the heart of an expanse of death, death in the heart of an expanse of life. True to its name, in the distance, the stark silhouette of Paris Mountain could be seen.

Alison coasted into the cemetery, following one of the narrow roads making up its circulatory system, maneuvering her way toward the far end where she pulled onto the soft earth next to a crumbling old cinderblock structure. Alison and Paul stepped out of the car and stood side-by-side, staring out across the graveyard. A carpet of grass so green it looked unreal, stone monuments and markers thrusting up like skyscrapers creating a city of the dead.

That's what cemeteries are, Alison ruminated, wryly amused by the curious poetical nature of her thoughts. *Cities of the dead.*

"Okay," Paul said, looking down at his tablet.

"According to what I found online, Lincoln's grave should be in the plot just to the right. Doesn't say what row it may be on, but the area isn't big and shouldn't take us long to find."

Alison nodded, and the two of them walked across the road, into one of the square plots. This particular plot contained maybe two dozen graves, and without a word, they split up, going from marker to marker, looking for the name Henry Lincoln etched in stone.

Alison stopped before a double headstone—Carl and Edna Gaffney, a sepia-toned oval-shaped portrait of the couple placed in the center of the marker—and stared up at the sky, a deepening blue, unblemished by clouds. She felt like an imbecile and an enabler, going along with Paul on this fool's errand. Her practical nature usually kept her out of such situations, yet . . .

As she stood there, feeling the rays of the dying sun warm her skin even as a gentle breeze ruffled her hair, she had to confess a twinge of excitement coursed through her like an electrical current. She was not a woman who sought out adventure, and while visiting a graveyard in the late afternoon could hardly be called a grand exploit in the vein of swashbucklers and Knights of the Round Table, it was still outside the parameters of her usual rigid routine. It felt good. It made her feel like life could be more than rules to follow and schedules to keep. She may never admit this out loud, but she could acknowledge it to herself.

"Here," she heard Paul call from a few feet away. Tearing herself from her own contemplations, she turned and made her way over to where he squatted in front of a large marble stone. HENRY ANDREW LINCOLN, and under his birth and death dates the inscription, "Now Gone on to the Greatest Mystery of All." The marker was old, chipped, and weathered, with an abstract mosaic of bird droppings splattered across the top, but the grave itself was well tended with a large wicker basket full of fresh roses set before it in an opulent display.

"What are the chances someone who died so long ago still has relatives bringing flowers to his grave?" she asked, hunkering down next to Paul.

Paul shrugged. "The man was a writer. Maybe he still has fans who like to pay their respects."

"That's possible," Alison said. "I think it's more likely those roses are meant for you. Look for a card."

Paul reached down and gently shifted through the flowers, being careful to avoid the thorns. Several of the bright red petals fluttered down to the grass like drops of blood. He sank his hands deeper into the blooms, knocking several of them out of the basket. He inhaled sharply through his teeth, and his posture went stiff as if he'd been turned to stone by glimpsing at Medusa.

Alison said, "What's wrong? Did you stick yourself with a thorn?"

He turned his head slowly to look at her, one corner of his mouth twitching. "It's not a card left for me."

"What do you mean?"

He slowly pulled his hands back out of the basket. He had in fact been pricked several times, fine jewels of blood bubbled up from the wounds, and an entire thorn stuck up from the pad of his thumb, but he didn't seem to notice. Truthfully, Alison only absently noticed herself; her attention was focused on the object held in Paul's scraped hands.

A book. A paperback with yellowed pages and a ripped cover, the binding split. If Alison had to guess, she'd say the book was older than Henry Lincoln's tombstone. Despite the faded nature of the cover, she could read the title and author. *The Color Purple* by Alice Walker.

"A thing of beauty," Paul said in a hush, the words tumbling out on his breath. He balanced the book in one palm, and with his other hand, he brushed his fingers reverently along the cover and the spine.

Alison found herself examining Paul's face, the almost spiritual rapture that lit his features. She'd seen this expression on him before but not since she'd first started working at the library. Alison loved books, and she loved her job, but for Paul, it seemed almost a religion.

For him, that would be Heaven. Instead of streets paved with gold, streets paved with pages.

"So what's our next clue?" she asked, making the decision that she was going to be by Paul's side through this no matter where it led them.

Gingerly, Paul opened the cover, trying not to rip it further. Nothing was written on the inside, so he thumbed through the pages. At the halfway point, just before the binding split, he found a small square card of thick stock with three words scrawled on it. He read them aloud to Alison.

She frowned. "What does that mean? Where do we go next?"

"I guess we don't make the next move," Paul said and looked back at the message on the card.

See you soon.

MUTINY

THEY PULLED BACK into the Super 8 parking lot only forty-five minutes after they'd left.

"Maybe Jasper won't even have noticed we were gone," Paul said from the passenger's seat.

Alison smiled at him. "Not likely. What are you going to tell him?"

"I won't be returning to Columbia with you. I realize it might mean my job, and I'll face those consequences if it comes to it, but my mind is made up. I'm staying."

"*We're* staying," Alison said.

Paul shook his head. "I can't ask you to do that."

"You didn't ask me; I'm offering. We still have no idea what's really going on here, but whatever it is, I'm not letting you walk into it alone."

"Alison, I need you back at the Library."

"Why?"

"If I do end up being fired, I want to know there's someone who actually cares about literature and preserving it for future generations to run things. If we both get the boot, it'll more than likely leave the Library in the hands of . . . "

"Jasper," Alison finished. "Joel would be there as a balancing influence."

Paul snorted. "In that couple, I think it's clear Jasper calls the shots. Joel has a lot of heart but no backbone. I need you to take the reins if this doesn't go my way, but believe me, I'm going to make my case passionately to Senator Kelley and the entire subcommittee. I'm not going without a fight."

"Good," Alison said, popping open the door. "And you know I'm on your side. What do you say we get inside and start strategizing?"

They walked in silence down the breezeway to Paul's room. He used his keycard to unlock the door then stopped abruptly in the threshold, causing Alison to nearly collide with his back.

"What's wrong?" she asked, but one glance over his shoulder gave her the answer.

J.J. waited inside Paul's room.

～﹀↙↙～

Jasper sat casually at the little round table in the corner, one foot resting on his knee, a lazy smile curling his lips. Joel stood next to the bed, looking uncomfortable and vaguely sick, like he'd eaten something bad and was just beginning to feel the effects of it.

"How did you get in my room?" Paul asked.

"I bribed the manager to let us in," Jasper said, picking lint off his pants, evincing an easy confidence as if he were holding court in his own office before subordinates and lackeys. "You'd be surprised how little it took. I guess managing a Super 8 doesn't pay a great deal."

Not trusting himself to speak, Paul kept his silence, knowing Jasper would eventually get to the point. The man loved the sound of his own voice.

"I came by your room about half an hour ago to see if you needed any help packing, and you weren't here. I then tried Ms. Wyatt's room, and she also wasn't here. Funny, when you both knew we were supposed to check out and head home."

"I had some errands to run; Alison tagged along."

"Errands, really? You mean like following the last clue Greg left behind?"

"It's not really any of your business."

"You're wrong. I promised Senator Kelley I'd make sure you followed orders, and I don't intend—" Jasper's words trailed off, his gaze dropping to Paul's side. "What is that?"

Paul looked down and saw Jasper staring at the book in his hand. "Talk about a dedicated employee," he said, holding the book out. "Greg is missing, and he's still making acquisitions for us."

"*The Color Purple*," Jasper read off the cover. "We already have that one."

"No, we don't. We have a restoration written by you but not the real thing."

"Some might say better than the real thing."

This statement stabbed at Paul like an icepick to the brain, but he refused to be baited. "Well, once we get this baby scanned into the system, we can delete the restoration."

"Maybe I should hang on to that," Jasper said.

Paul felt his fingers tightening possessively on the book. "Why?"

"The cover looks like it's about to fall off. We should probably get it sealed up in a bag."

"What do you care?" Alison spoke up from behind Paul. She'd stepped inside but left the door open, as if anticipating the need for a quick getaway. "You seem to think your version of the novel is superior to Ms. Walker's anyway, so why are you so worried about preserving it?"

"Excessive damage decreases the value," Jasper said and winced, as if the sharp edge of honesty in his words sliced into his tongue.

Paul frowned. "Value? What? Are you a Book Hound now? Looking to sell?"

Jasper glanced over at his husband, his expression yelling, *Jump in and lend me a hand anytime*, but Joel just walked across the room and disappeared through the door into the bathroom. Turning back to Paul and Alison, Jasper forced a strained smile, which looked more like a grimace. "I don't know what has gotten into everybody, but I seem to be the only one thinking rationally here."

"That so?" Paul said. "Because I'd say you're more like a petulant teenager who thinks he knows more than he does and is playing at being a grownup."

A pink blush crept up from Jasper's collar like a rash, rapidly working its way up his neck and face until his entire countenance was painted in fuchsia. When he spoke, his voice was soft but heated, a lethal hiss. "Is that so, Mr. Hotshot? We'll see if you still feel the same when I'm doing your job and doing it a million times better."

Joel came back into the room carrying the water glass that had been sitting wrapped in plastic next to the sink, sloshingly full. He held the glass out to Jasper. "Sweetie, just try to calm down and drink a little water."

"I don't want to calm down," Jasper spat, turning on his husband. "And I don't want any fucking water!"

Joel didn't respond with anger or hurt, simply a patient smile. Paul thought the man must be some kind of saint. "Jasper, please, for me. Just have a sip and take a minute before you say anything else. I don't want to see this situation get any nastier."

At first, it appeared like Jasper would ignore his husband's request, but then he took the glass and downed the water in three long gulps. He stood for a moment, taking several deep breaths, clutching the glass so tightly Paul wouldn't have been surprised if it had shattered in his hand.

"Okay," Jasper said, his voice still strained but the tone much more reasonable and measured. "Joel's right; there's no reason for us to be at each other's throats. Let's just get back to Columbia, and we can work all this out."

"I'm not going back," Paul said, the announcement falling like a stone down a deep well.

"You *have* to go back," Jasper said, his words infused less with anger than weariness.

"I'm a grown man. I don't see how I have to do anything I don't want to."

"Senator Kelley gave specific orders to—"

"The senator is not my father or my master, and I'm certainly not his child or his slave. Therefore, I don't really think he is in any position to order me around."

"He's your boss."

"Well, Paul is your boss," Alison said.

Jasper turned his attention to her. "What about you? You staying as well?"

"No, with Paul here in Greer, I'll be needed to run things back at the Library."

Jasper laughed, the sound harsh and brittle. "What makes you think you'll be running things?"

Paul said, "Enough! I'm staying here; that's settled. You three can head back home and meet with Senator Kelley in the morning. Alison can explain my stance, and if he wants to talk to me, he knows my number."

"Fine," Jasper said, his left eyelid drooping as if he had a sty. "But I'm taking that book with me."

"I don't think I trust you with it. I'll let Alison take it with her."

"Listen here—" Jasper took a step forward, but his knees seemed to give in, and he would have fallen if Joel hadn't been there to catch him. The glass slipped from his hand and landed on the carpet with a soft *thud*.

"You okay?" Joel asked.

Jasper shook his husband off. "Nothing wrong with me except I'm tired of all this nonsense." His words were slurred.

If Paul didn't know any better, he would have sworn the man was drunk.

Jasper swayed on his feet, slapped himself lightly on the cheeks a couple of times, and shook his head. "I just—I just need to—I don't know—"

He toppled again, but Joel was there, propping him up and leading him over to the bed, where they both sat on the edge of the mattress.

"Just take it easy," Joel said soothingly.

Jasper fumbled a hand at his ear. "Senator Kelley is expecting us . . . " *Shenator Kelley ishpecting ush . . .*

Joel plucked the bulb from his husband's ear and pocketed it. "You don't need that. You just need to get some rest."

Jasper looked at Joel, but his head bobbed and his chin kept hitting his chest. He couldn't seem to keep his eyes open.

"*Whashappening?*"

"You're exhausted," Joel said and kissed his husband on the temple. "You'll feel better after you sleep."

Gently, Joel leaned Jasper back until the man was reclined on the bed. He lifted his legs and turned him so that his entire body was on the mattress. Loud, frog-like snores issued from his gaping mouth.

Paul and Alison had crept to the foot of the bed. "What the hell is going on?" Paul demanded.

After smoothing back the hair off his husband's sweaty forehead, Jasper straightened up and faced Paul. "I dosed his water with a strong sedative. He should be out for a couple of hours."

"Why?" Alison asked.

"We need time to discuss some things."

Paul felt totally adrift, as if nothing in the world made sense anymore. "What sorts of things?"

"Earlier, you jokingly asked Jasper if he was a Book Hound."

"Wait," Paul said, feeling like he may need to lie down himself. "Are you saying I was right? Jasper's a Book Hound?"

Joel took a deep breath and said, "No, he's not, but I am."

JOEL'S SECRET

THE THREE OF them sat around the table. Paul and Alison close together and Joel across from them. On the bed, Jasper rolled onto his side, passed gas, and continued snoring.

"So I'm sure you have lots of questions," Joel said, his demeanor one of unperturbed calm.

Paul laughed a dry, humorless laugh. "That's an understatement."

"I'm ready to come clean, so whatever you want to know, just ask."

What Paul really wanted to do was reach across the table, grab Joel, and shake him. He'd always considered Joel a timid mouse of a person, but he'd been a traitor all this time. A double agent.

He took a breath and said, "So, have you been a Book Hound the entire time you've worked for me?"

"Yes."

"Have you acquired books from the Library itself?"

"On occasion."

The urge to grab Joel increased, but Alison put a hand on his arm and said, her voice tight, "I guess you've made quite a pretty penny in the last couple of years."

"I'm not in it for money."

Paul and Alison exchanged a puzzled glance, and Paul said, "I don't understand. That's what Book Hounds do. They find books and sell them to the highest bidder."

"That's what *most* Book Hounds do but not my group. We are not interested in profit; we're interested in preservation."

"Your *group*?" Alison said. "So you work for an organization?"

"I wouldn't call it an organization. We're just likeminded individuals with a common goal, to amass and preserve as many books as we can. To date, we've collected close to five-thousand volumes."

Paul and Alison glanced at one another again, and he could see the same thought surfacing in her eyes. He turned back to Joel and gave voice to it. "Are you saying you're part of Book Haven?"

Joel's mouth twisted in a wry smile. "That's not a name we ascribe to ourselves, but it's how we're commonly known, yes."

"How exactly did you get involved with this group?"

"I'm one of the founders."

Paul had never been dumbstruck before, but he found himself so now. He wasn't entirely sure he believed any of this, but it was a damn good story. "So, you . . . you're one of the founders of Book Haven?"

Joel shrugged, as if it were news no more astonishing than if he'd announced he had had steak for dinner the previous evening. "It started as a network of people connected online, talking about our love of literature and our desire to preserve it as well as our distrust of the government's ability to do so.

Though we have yet to find any concrete proof and many would call us conspiracy theorists, we believe that it is at least possible the government is responsible for the Wipe itself."

"Yet you joined the Library," Paul said.

"Well, we figured it would be smart to get some men on the inside, see how the government was running their show. So, a few of us got jobs at different facilities throughout the country. Of course, when Jasper insisted on applying as well, it made things a little more difficult for me."

Alison looked over at the still form on the bed. "Jasper has no idea that you're involved in any of this?"

Joel shook his head. "I doubt he'd approve. Besides, he's had his own clandestine activities to keep him occupied."

Paul wondered what Joel meant, but he decided to let it go for now. "In the years you've been working for the Library, what have you determined?"

"That our initial assumption was correct. The government can't be trusted with the preservation of literature."

"What do you mean?"

"Come on, Mr. Nelson, you know as well as I do the government is on track to do away with the Acquisitions Department altogether. They want to focus solely on Restoration. Not only is it less costly but it actually *makes* the government money. They own the rights to all the restorations, which means they make a profit on every book sold. Why would they want to bother paying for manuscripts that won't make them a dime? We realized we were pretty much alone in this fight, so we decided to up our recruitment. That's where you come in."

Paul started, as if a firecracker had gone off next to him. "Me? You want to recruit *me*?"

"That's what this is all about, why we brought you here."

"You didn't bring me here. I came because—"

Paul's words cut off abruptly as the ramifications of what Joel suggested sank in. Alison seemed to pick up on it too. "You're saying Greg is involved in this?" she asked.

Joel nodded. "I recruited him myself. He's been playing both sides of the fence for the past six months. For every book he has procured for the Library on his acquisition trips, he has procured two for us. And we have snuck some back out of the vault after they've been uploaded to the database."

"I can't believe it," Paul said. "I thought Greg was my friend."

"He is, which is why he recommended we bring you onboard. He told us about your copy of *Great Expectations*, which certainly was a plus as far as we were concerned."

Paul felt Alison's piercing stare but ignored it. "Why all this rigmarole with the clues and everything?"

"Frankly, Greg believed you would be receptive to what we were doing, but others of us weren't so sure. We needed time to monitor you, get a feel for how you would deal with the idea that Book Haven might be more than a myth. Then you called in Alison, Jasper, and me, which complicated things further, but we were able to glean from how you've handled things here that you might have what it takes to be one of us."

"What about me?" Alison asked.

"For you, we have other plans."

Paul opened his mouth to speak when there was a knock at the door. He bolted to his feet, knocking his chair to the carpet. "Who the hell is that?"

Joel, unruffled, said, "I think it's probably for you."

Alison, tense in her chair, shook her head, but Paul cautiously approached the door. Leaning forward, he put his eye to the peephole. When he saw the figure standing outside in the breezeway, he tore open the door and engulfed the man in a hug.

Laughing, Greg Nylon squeezed him and said, "Told you I'd see you soon, Willie."

THE REAL LIBRARY

THEY PULLED OUT of the parking lot in Paul's car. Greg drove with Paul in the passenger's seat, Alison and Joel in the back. They'd left Jasper sleeping in Paul's room.

Paul kept staring at Greg, afraid his friend might disappear again. "You know I've been worried sick about you, you bastard."

"Hey, it wasn't my idea to handle things this way," Greg said with a pointed glance over his shoulder into the backseat. Joel said nothing, just gazed out the window.

"What about that phone call I made to you? You sounded like you were being chased."

"Part of the plan, window dressing. We wanted to make sure you were concerned enough that you'd come when the sheriff called you."

"Well, it worked. A little too well."

Greg's grip on the steering wheel tightened, and his face became both serious and sad. "I'm sorry, truly. If it'd been up to me, I'd have just told you what was going on, but I'm still pretty low on the totem pole here."

"So, what's your end game?" Paul asked, deciding to cut the guilt trip. "I mean, you've been officially reported missing. What next?"

"Simple, I'm finally going to contact you, drunk as a skunk. The story will be that I've been covering up a serious drinking problem and went on a weeklong bender, which I can barely recall, have been staying with some woman I met out at a bar. In about a week or so, I'll tender my resignation."

"Your resignation?" Alison exclaimed from the backseat. "You're going to quit the Library?"

Joel answered for Greg. "We're going to start pulling our people out. It's getting to the point where there's not much more we can do from the inside."

Paul started to speak, but then Greg said, "Just be patient for a few more minutes. When we get where we're going, you'll have all the answers."

Alison leaned forward, popping her head between the two front seats. "Where exactly are you taking us? Book Haven?"

"In a sense," Greg said.

Paul knew he wasn't going to get any more information out of Greg, so he stopped asking and remained silent the rest of the way. They turned off Wade Hampton onto Middleton Way. A few blocks down, they crossed through a large intersection onto Pennsylvania Avenue, where they then pulled into an empty parking lot.

Staring out the windshield, Paul examined the building ahead. A large, triangular, brick structure with a tall, peaked arch over the entrance. The brick was weathered and chipped, and the entire place had a shabbiness to it that suggested it hadn't been used in years. Perhaps decades. On the right side of the building were several thin, rectangular windows, two of them boarded over with plywood.

"What is this place?" Alison whispered.

Releasing his seatbelt, Joel said, "In the distant past, this was an actual library full of books for the public to check out. Most recently, it was used as offices for the local school district, but that was almost twenty years ago now. It has been abandoned since then, but a member of our group owns it and lets us utilize it for our purposes."

As the four of them exited the car, Paul noticed the lot wasn't completely deserted as he'd first thought. The sky was a deep velvety purple sprinkled with tiny pinpricks of light, and under the deeper shade of a Magnolia tree at the very far end of the lot was a dark-colored pick-up truck.

Following his gaze, Joel said, "You'll be meeting a few of the other founders."

Approaching the entrance, Paul felt trepidation fluttering in his stomach. This whole cloak-and-dagger setup unnerved him, and he wondered if he should be following along so blindly. He had thought he knew Greg and Joel, but now he realized they might as well be strangers. Could he trust they weren't the enemy?

Greater than the trepidation was a childlike excitement he could only think to describe in terms of clichés. A kid on Christmas morning, a teenager about to get his driver's license, a man about to make love for the first time. If Joel were to be believed, this building housed five-thousand volumes under its roof. The thought of being in the midst of so much literature made Paul giddy, almost breathless, with anticipation.

Joel went first. He typed in a code on a small touchscreen set next to the door then scanned a keycard. The lock disengaged with a loud and ominous *clunk*! The door slid open on a track, and Paul noticed it opened smoothly with not so much as a squeak. The building may look rundown, but someone took care of it.

Next to Paul, Alison studied the grounds. "You ever think of putting out any 'No Trespassing' signs?" she asked.

Joel shook his head. "That kind of stuff would only draw vagrants and teens looking for a place to screw around. Our goal is to have the building blend in to the point where it practically becomes invisible."

Joel led them inside, and Paul found himself in a wide, dimly-lit vestibule that led to another locked door. Once they were through, they came out into an open area with offices opening along the perimeter. The space reminded him of the bullpen at the Library where all the restoration artists worked in their cubicles, only this area was completely empty except for a scarred wooden conference table in the center. It looked like it could easily seat a dozen people, but there were only seven chairs at the table, the metal folding kind. In two of these chairs sat an older man with gray hair and a young woman of maybe twenty. A third person leaned against the edge of the table, his arms folded across his chest.

Stunned, Paul said, "Sheriff Stevens?"

ALL ON THE TABLE

OUT OF HIS UNIFORM, Bryant Stevens looked different. Paul couldn't pinpoint exactly how, but he seemed even leaner, his face somehow more nondescript. The uniform had lent him an air of authority that made one take notice, but in civilian attire of faded jeans and a white T-shirt, there was nothing about him that stood out. The kind of person one might pass on the street and not even register. Perhaps like the building, he hoped to become practically invisible.

"Good to see you again, Mr. Nelson," he said. "You as well, Ms. Wyatt."

Recovering from the shock of seeing the sheriff here, Paul said, "So you're in on this too? You're certainly a hell of an actor."

"I could say the same about you. I studied you closely when you found Greg's message on the title page of *Alice's Adventures in Wonderland*, and if I hadn't known you were lying when you said you couldn't read it, I would have sworn you were telling the truth."

"You're all great liars, Joel and Greg included," Alison said, walking to the table and taking a seat at the far end.

Paul followed and sat next to her, Joel and Greg joining them. They sat on one side of the table across from the older man and younger woman, who still had not spoken. Stevens took the only chair left, at the very head of the table.

"Is this where you make your pitch?" Paul asked the sheriff.

"First, I think I'll make introductions. This is Bianca," he said, gesturing toward the young woman. "She's our resident computer expert. Next to her is Charles, the owner of this building and generous benefactor for a lot of our operations, at least on the local level."

Charles shrugged. "My grandparents made a fortune in robotic technology. I am more than happy to put the family's money to good use."

"I see. Well, I'm—"

"We know who you are, Mr. Nelson," Bianca said with a sardonic twist of her mouth. "We've sort of been keeping tabs on you."

"Of course. I've been tapped for recruitment."

"That's right," Stevens said.

"How many people do you have working for you?"

The sheriff chuckled. "You make it sound like we run a business."

"What would you call it? A nonprofit?"

"If you insist on calling us something, preservationists I think cuts closest to the heart of our mission statement."

"And what exactly is your mission statement?" Alison asked.

Stevens turned his tender smile on her. "Simply to provide a haven for books."

"Joel told me you're planning to start pulling your people out of the Libraries," Paul said. "So, why are you recruiting from within?"

Stevens folded his arms on the tabletop and leaned forward. "What we look for in a recruit is someone who is passionate about literature, specifically passionate about the preservation of literature. That definitely describes you. The fact that you have a history degree helps, as does your having held such a high position within the government. You know how government officials think, and it could prove invaluable. Not to mention how you've kept that copy of *Great Expectations* for yourself. It certainly worked in your favor. All of this was compelling, but it really was your behavior since you arrived here in Greer that decided us on reaching out to you."

"How so?"

"When you hid the clues from me, when you didn't report what was going on here to Senator Kelley and the Subcommittee, when you decided to risk your job in the pursuit of Book Haven . . . that's how we knew you possessed the other key characteristic we look for in a recruit."

Paul raised an eyebrow.

Stevens leaned over even further so that he was practically coming out of his seat. "A deep-seeded conviction that the government can't be trusted to preserve literature. Because they don't want to, aren't even interested in doing so."

Paul wanted to deny this, to tell Stevens he was wrong, but the sheriff spoke the truth. Over the past couple of years, Paul's belief in the work they were doing at the Library had eroded and crumbled to dust.

In theory, it should have been a noble endeavor, but the red-tape and bureaucracy continued to increase, impeding any substantive progress. Paul had thought of himself as a modern day Sisyphus, constantly pushing a rock up the hill only to have it slide back down and crush him.

"What is my part in all this?" Alison said, mimicking her earlier question back in the motel when Joel had said they had other plans for her. "Have you had your eye on me for recruitment as well?"

"Actually no," Stevens said. "Quite frankly, you weren't really on our radar. It was Joel who convinced us to bring you in."

Alison turned to Joel. "What did I do to make the cut?"

Joel said, "When you decided to go with Mr. Nelson to the cemetery to search for the next clue. You've always been hard to read, and I didn't know if you had it in you to break the rules even for a greater good, but in that moment, I saw something in you to the contrary."

"So you want me to become a preservationist as well?"

"We're hoping," Stevens said, "you'll be our woman on the inside at the Library."

Paul found himself confused, having trouble following the twists and turns of this conversation. "I thought that was what you wanted me for, to be your man on the inside."

"I'm afraid you're not going to be on the inside much longer," Stevens said.

"What are you talking about?"

"Joel, why don't you explain the situation to our guests?"

Joel placed his tablet on the table and began tapping at the screen. "Recently, I've noticed suspicious behavior from Jasper. Late night calls and messages, secrecy, a sort of agitated nervousness. I'm sure you noticed his growing ambition. I tried not to think the worst, but shortly after you two left for the cemetery, I contacted Bianca and had her hack into Jasper's accounts."

Joel said all this with a detached casualness belied by the hurt in his eyes.

Hurt and guilt, Paul thought.

"What did you find out?" Alison asked.

Joel slid the tablet over so she and Paul could both see the screen. Several documents were open in a grid; Paul only had to tap on one to enlarge it.

"These are emails, text messages, and there are even audio files for a couple of undeleted voicemails," Joel said. "It would seem that for the past year, Jasper has been in regular contact with Senator Kelley, and the two have been discussing the government's plans for the Libraries."

Paul was studying an email sent from Kelley to Jasper, and it felt as if a cork in the bottom of his foot had been removed, draining all the warmth out of him. He raised his head slowly, his mouth dry and his hands shaking.

"They're planning to abolish the Acquisitions department?" he said in a hollow voice.

Joel nodded. "Apparently. It would still have to be approved by Congress, but I have no doubt it'll pass easily in the current political climate. This would put the control of literature solely in the government's hands. They'd be making all the money and could control the content. There would be nothing to stop

Jasper or those who think like him from 'improving' classic works."

"What about all the books we've already acquired that are stored in the vaults?" Alison asked as she opened more documents on the tablet.

"They plan to clean out the vaults," Bianca said. "Sell off the inventory to wealthy private collectors. It will make the government even more money while allowing the general public access to only the government-owned restorations."

Paul shook his head, as if the simple act could somehow negate the truth of what he'd heard. "I won't stand for this."

"You won't be in a position to do anything about it," Stevens said.

"Enough with the cryptic statements. Just tell me what you're talking about."

Alison gasped softly then held the tablet up to him. "I think he's talking about this."

Paul took the tablet and scanned the document, a screenshot of a text exchange between Jasper and Kelley earlier in the evening.

Kelley: Nelson is becoming a problem.

Jasper: This situation with Nylon has got him acting very irrational. I agree, the man is a liability.

Kelley: This goes back further than Nylon's disappearance. Nelson's behavior has been troublesome for some time now. He cares too much for the books themselves, it blinds him to the big picture.

Jasper: Exactly. He is an impediment to what we hope to achieve. If we really want to make progress, we need to remove him.

Kelley: That is already in the works. Everyone on the Subcommittee agrees the Southeastern Library needs a new director.

Jasper: You know I would be honored for the opportunity.

Kelley: I will recommend you for the job, but it may be an uphill battle. Wyatt is preferred by most of the other members because of her experience and dedication.

Jasper: No one at that Library is more dedicated than I am.

Kelley: Perhaps, but you have a reputation as being a bit stubborn and opinionated. The Subcommittee is looking for someone they can rely on to simply follow orders without question.

Jasper: That is not Ms. Wyatt. It only seems that way because she agrees with Nelson on every little thing. I don't know if they are really just that alike or she's in love with him or something, but I'm not so sure how well she'd follow orders given by anyone else.

Kelley: It will be taken into consideration, believe me, just as soon as Nelson is terminated.

Paul had read enough. He shoved the tablet away from him with his fingertips. He felt as if someone had split him open, scooped out his insides, then sewed him back up. Leaving him completely hollowed out. His relationship with the Subcommittee had become contentious and the job at times a burden, yet his work was how he defined himself. What was he without it? He'd always thought he was good at what he did, and it hurt to know there were some conspiring against him.

But, he told himself, those conspiring against him were not interested in the work he had signed on for. Preserving the world's literature was no longer the business they were in. If Paul wanted to continue that mission, he'd have to find somewhere else to do it.

His hands lay on the tabletop, and he noticed they shook slightly. Earlier, while still outside the building, he had felt the excitement of a young man on the brink of losing his virginity; now, he felt the combination of fear and expectation that comes with someone filing for divorce or applying for his first mortgage. The feeling of standing on the precipice of a major life change. Terrified to take the leap while exhilarated at the prospect of the freefall.

"What do I do?" he asked, staring down at his trembling hands.

NEW ARRANGEMENTS

"YOU'LL GO BACK to Columbia and be fired," Stevens said matter-of-factly. "You'll go through the motions of putting up a fight, but the decision has already been made, and you will be terminated. At that point, you'll return to Greer and take a job working for the sheriff's department."

"The sheriff's department? What kind of work would I do with the sheriff's department?"

"The price of antique books has become so high that independent Book Hounds have begun to engage in some, shall we say, unscrupulous behavior to obtain them. Burglary, assault, blackmail, intimidation. I believe it's a serious enough problem that I've decided to institute a taskforce specifically to combat those crimes. I will be offering you and Mr. Nylon the opportunity to head up the taskforce."

Paul glanced over at Greg, who smiled back at him. "It's the perfect cover, and we can use our expertise and contacts to track down as many books as possible before the government gets to them."

"I'm confused," Alison said. "I thought the government was going to do away with Acquisitions."

"There is correspondence in the documents we secured," Stevens said, pointing toward the tablet, "indicating the government's plans to form its own army of Book Hounds to obtain volumes for profit."

"So there will still be an Acquisitions budget?" Paul asked.

Stevens tilted his head and gave him a look of mixed amusement and affection, the kind of look a parent gives a child who has asked a question of such innocent naivety that the purity is touching. "There are a million ways the government can seize property from citizens. They've been doing it for centuries."

Greg said, "That's why it's imperative we get there first."

Alison cleared her throat, and all eyes turned to her. "Is that why you need me on the inside?"

Stevens smiled. "Very perceptive. Yes, we need someone in a position of authority within the Library who can feed us information when the government has pinpointed a cache of books they hope to acquire. Our budget may have its limits, but hopefully if we can get there first, we'll be able to secure the books before the government can get the paperwork together to confiscate them."

"Aren't you worried they'll trace the purchases back to you and discover what you're doing here?"

"Leave that to me," Bianca said. "I know how to cover our tracks."

Alison nodded, seemed to mull it over, before answering, "Okay, I'll do it."

"It won't be easy," Joel said. "Jasper is going to fight for the job, and he fights dirty. However, we know that you are the preferred candidate. We just have to make sure you stay that way."

"Meaning?"

"You have to turn against me," Paul said, following the logic.

"Turn on you? How?"

Joel answered. "You'll have to go before the Subcommittee and tell them that Mr. Nelson's actions here in Greer were irrational and unprofessional, and that you don't think he is fit to lead the Southeastern Library any longer. You'll also have to be convincing. If they have any inkling that you sympathize with him, you might be passed over for someone they *know* they have in their pocket."

"Once this is all done," Greg said, "you'll have to cut off direct contact with Paul and me. It would look too suspicious otherwise."

"But how will I communicate any information I obtain?"

"I'll set you up with a secured encrypted server," Bianca said. "You'll be able to use it to send us messages, though don't expect any responses."

"Is this happening all over the country?" Alison asked.

"We have operatives placed within practically every Library facility," Stevens said. "However, almost all of them are in low-level positions and will be pulled out over the course of the next year. You will be the jewel in our crown, so to speak."

Joel took his tablet back and glanced at the top of the screen. "Ms. Wyatt, we really need to get going."

"Going? Going where?"

"Jasper won't be out for much longer. Charles is going to run us back to the motel so we'll be there when he wakes up."

"What are you going to tell him?" Paul asked.

"A little bit of truth to make the lies easier to swallow. I'm going to tell him I put a sedative in his water because I felt the situation was becoming too volatile, and while he was unconscious, you finally got a message from Mr. Nylon—"

"Which I will insert onto your tablet along with the appropriate timestamp," Bianca said.

"—and you left to go get him. Ms. Wyatt will be upset, explaining that she went with you to the cemetery only to try to talk some sense into you, to no avail. The three of us will leave for Columbia, and you and Greg will follow tomorrow to face the consequences of your actions."

Everything was happening so fast, it left Paul feeling a little dizzy. He was about to step over the point of no return, and nothing in his life was ever going to be the same after this. However, he found himself in this moment thinking not of the ramifications for his life. "Jasper isn't going to be too happy when he finds out you sedated him," he said to Joel. "Aren't you worried this could cause irreparable damage to your marriage?"

Joel's expression was blank, but his eyes were bottomless pits of sorrow. "I think that ship has already sailed."

Paul wanted to offer some words of comfort, but there were none sufficient to express his feelings, so he kept his silence. Joel looked away and then rose from his chair. As if this was some silent cue, everyone else stood as well.

Alison and Paul stared at one another, and a heaviness settled on his shoulders like a wet blanket. He wasn't sure who moved first; it almost seemed as if neither of them had. Just one second they were standing face-to-face, and the next they were embracing.

He could feel Alison's warm breath on his neck as she spoke. "Paul, I can't believe this is it. I want you to know how much I've always respected you, and I'm going to miss you."

"We're going to see one another back in Columbia," he said, but he understood how empty those words were. Though they may only be acting, when they saw one another again, they would appear to be on opposite sides. Enemies. This would be the last time they'd meet as friends and colleagues. He squeezed her a little tighter, something he'd never have considered when they were coworkers. However, that term no longer applied; now they were *coconspirators*.

They pulled apart, and Paul thought he might have detected tears in Alison's eyes, but she turned away too quickly to be sure. She hurried back to the vestibule, Charles following along behind her. Joel hesitated before he held out his hand. He and Paul shook without speaking, not as emotional a goodbye as the one he'd shared with Alison but somehow just as significant.

That left just four standing around the conference table. Paul looked to Greg and said, "What do we do now?"

"We'll wait a while, then you'll call Senator Kelley and explain how you've located me at the home of a local woman where I've been shacked up for the last several days."

"That would be me," Bianca said.

Paul laughed. "Greg, don't you think you might be robbing the cradle a little?"

"What can I say, Nelson?" Greg said with a sly smile. "The young chicks dig me."

"That's a load of dreck if I've ever heard one."

"Actually," Bianca said, stepping around the table to stand next to Greg, taking his hand, "it's not."

"Oh."

Greg shrugged and said, "It's very new." The way he brought her hand up to kiss the back of it, combined with the smitten look in his eyes, told Paul that while it may be new, it was also powerful.

Stevens came up next to him, and for an absurd moment, Paul wondered if the sheriff was going to take his hand as well. Instead, he clamped a hand on Paul's shoulder and said, "Mr. Nelson, I know this is a lot to take in. You must have more questions."

"First of all, you can start calling me Paul."

"Of course, and you can call me Bryant."

"Second, I have an avalanche of questions that will probably bury you alive, but I'll start with just one. Can I see the books?"

"That's a good opening question. Follow me."

Stevens led Paul to one of the office doors to the right of them. This was the only office inside the building that required a keycard and a code to enter. The door opened inward into a large, dark room, so dark it was like they were entering a black hole in the deepest reaches of space. Stevens flipped a switch, and the room flooded with light.

Paul guessed this had once been a conference room of some type, long but narrow. In the far wall, two thin, rectangular windows were covered over with thick, black plastic. The walls were lined with metal bookshelves that stretched up to the ceiling, and the interior was a maze of shorter wooden bookcases.

Every inch of space was filled with books. Hardcovers, paperbacks, some in almost pristine conditions and others held together with tape and string. The air was redolent with the musty, spicy scent of old pages. Paul breathed it in and felt his lungs inflate with history and art and passion. He stepped into the room, moving slowly, feeling the reverence and awe that cathedrals usually produced in the devout.

Stopping before a waist-high bookcase, he noted this one contained what seemed to be a complete *Oz* series. He reached out a hand then stayed it, looking back at the sheriff. "Can I touch one?"

"Of course. Those are some of our newest acquisitions."

Paul took the first book off the top shelf, *The Wonderful Wizard of Oz*, and opened it, flipping through the pages. The volume was oddly bloated, the pages slightly discolored and brittle as if it had gotten wet sometime in the past, but all the text seemed legible, a fantasy world springing to life between two covers.

"Where are the rest?" he asked, returning the book to its proper place.

"These are all the books housed in this building."

Paul scanned the room again. If he had to estimate, he'd say there were between two hundred to two hundred and fifty books on these shelves. "Joel told us that you all had collected around five thousand books."

"True, but they are not all in one location. It would be too dangerous. Like the Libraries, we have locations and operatives all over the country. As well as a few in Canada and even some in Europe. Book Haven isn't a specific place; it's an idea, a mission."

Paul nodded. "Speaking of mission, you said your mission statement was the preservation of literature, but who exactly are we preserving it for if it remains hidden away?"

"We're preserving it for future generations. I believe someday people will wake up and realize they deserve better than the pale imitations the government provides. They'll demand the richness of the originals, and when they do, we'll be there."

Paul felt a smile stretching across his face like a banner. "I like the sound of that, and I'm happy to be a part of it."

He followed Stevens out of the room.

Article from the Columbia, South Carolina online news source, **The State:**

A major shakeup has happened in the leadership of the Southeastern Institute of Acquisition and Restoration of Literature after losing two high-ranking officials in the past few days.

Head of Acquisitions, Gregory Nylon, resigned after admitting to alcoholism and disappearing for several days during a routine field assignment. Following a short in-house inquiry, Paul Nelson, who has run the Southeastern Institute since its inception, has been terminated for gross negligence and insubordination resulting from his mishandling of the investigation into Nylon's disappearance. His former assistant, Alison Wyatt, has been named his successor.

Nor will these personnel changes be the only major overhaul. Senator Roger Kelley, majority leader of the Senate Subcommittee which oversees all

Institutes throughout the country, announced in a press conference yesterday afternoon that the name of the Institutes will be rechristened the Institutes for Restoration of Literature. The costly Acquisitions program will be phased out as the government places its focus solely on Restoration instead.

"By narrowing our concentration and no longer dividing our efforts, we will be able to make more books available to the public at a much quicker pace," Kelley said. "I think the public will agree that this will be a win for all lovers of literature."

THE NEW GUARD

JASPER BARGED INTO Alison's office without knocking. As usual.

Alison swallowed the sharp words that rose to her lips like jagged pieces of broken glass shredding her esophagus. She gnashed her teeth and tried to make it look like a smile. She could still feel the resentment wafting off Jasper like a blast of heat. After six months, he still had not gotten over the fact that she got the position he wanted, but he had gotten a promotion. He was Alison's assistant.

Or babysitter, she thought would be a more appropriate title. His job was to make sure she didn't step out of line. She forced herself to remain calm and polite no matter how rude or condescending he became.

"Susie says you still haven't approved her restoration of *Gone with the Wind*!" Jasper barked at her.

"Good morning to you, too, Jasper. How was your weekend?"

"If you insist on these phony pleasantries, my weekend was crap. I got the final divorce papers from Joel."

"Oh," Alison said, feeling like the world's biggest

ass. Jasper and Joel had split up shortly after they returned from Greer, and Joel had transferred to a Library on the West Coast. So now J.J. was only J.

"I'd ask you about your personal life," Jasper said with a sneer, "but I know you don't have one. How about instead you tell me why you're refusing to approve *Gone with the Wind*? It was submitted to you last Wednesday."

"I'm not refusing to approve anything. I'm simply swamped is all. Since they increased the number of restoration artists, I'm getting close to fifty restorations a week. It takes me a while to get through all the files."

"You wouldn't have that problem if you'd simply authorize me to approve restorations myself."

"I value your opinion," Alison said evenly; this was one of those instances where she had to tread carefully. "I read all your notes and recommendations and take them into consideration, but I still have to go through each individual restoration and approve it myself. Otherwise, what am I here for?"

"Good question," Jasper mumbled but loud enough for Alison to hear.

Ignoring the insubordination, Alison said, "I'll get to it today; I promise."

She had hoped this would satisfy him enough to leave her office, but instead, he remained rooted in place, his arms folded across his chest. "Your procrastination wouldn't have anything to do with the fact that I personally oversaw this restoration, giving Susie guidelines on the new ending, would it?"

"Jasper, I haven't even read the restoration yet, but knowing you, I would guess the new ending involves

Rhett forgiving Scarlet and them riding off into the sunset to live happily ever after."

"It's what the reading public wants."

Alison folded her hands on the desktop and leaned forward. "Look, I am completely on board with the new directives that have come down from the Subcommittee. I understand our mission."

"Really? I seem to recall you getting quite upset back when I tried to alter the ending of *Romero and Juliet*."

"We had different directives then."

"And you're all about following orders, aren't you?"

Alison didn't take the bait, just stared at him in silence.

"How's Paul?" he asked abruptly.

"I haven't spoken to Mr. Nelson since he was terminated after the fiasco in Greer."

"We seem to remember your actions in Greer differently."

"Jasper," she sighed, finally letting the exasperation color her voice, "I have a lot of work to do. If you truly want me to get to *Gone with the Wind* today, I suggest you let me get to it."

At first, he didn't move, but finally, he turned and left the office, not bothering to close the door behind him.

Alison crossed the room and pushed the door shut. This double-agent-behind-enemy-lines life she led was tougher than she'd ever imagined it would be, and she hadn't expected it to be easy.

Returning to her desk, she picked up her tablet and checked her work email. More restoration files had been sent to her as well as a mass email from Senator

Kelley to all the top Library officials. The email detailed more changes to come—the emptying of the vaults was to begin soon—as well as updates about other projects. A section near the end caught her attention.

> We have located a rare collection of Poe and Lovecraft, owned by a wealthy family in Charleston, SC. Luckily, the oldest son, Edward Phelps, has recently been accused of assaulting a young woman at a college. We are in the process of obtaining the proper warrants to search the property and seize any materials that may seem pertinent to the case. The argument could be made that such dark reading material could have contributed to the assault. Once we have the books in our possession—

Alison stopped reading, disgusted. The government was pouncing on the personal tragedies and hardships of its citizens in order to fill their own coffers. Was this Edward Phelps guilty of the assault he was accused of? Perhaps, perhaps not . . . it didn't matter to Senator Kelley or the other members of the Subcommittee as long as it helped them get what they wanted.

She reached down to rummage through her purse beside her chair and retrieved a mini-tablet, about the size of an old-time cellular telephone. She'd received it five months ago in an unmarked package with no return address or postage. It was just sitting on her doorstep. It could send messages but not receive any.

She quickly typed in the text from the email regarding the impending seizure of the Phelps family's books, keeping the mini-tablet below the edge of the desk. As soon as she was done, she hit send and then tossed the machine back into her purse. Her heart pounded in her chest, and sweat trickled down the sides of her face. Part of her felt like she was doing something shameful and wicked.

I am *doing something illegal.*

Another part of her felt like what she was doing was right. Noble even. Despite the stress that came with her new position, exhilaration coursed through her body, and she knew it was worth the risk.

Her smile faltered only slightly as she opened the file for the desecrated *Gone with the Wind* restoration.

—✦—

Paul and Greg backed the truck up to the entrance of the headquarters. Stevens and Charles waited to help them unload the boxes. Six altogether, filled with the works of Edgar Allen Poe, H.P. Lovecraft, even some Stephen King and Clive Barker.

"Any trouble?" Stevens asked.

"A little haggling over the price, but we finally settled on twenty thousand for the lot," Greg said.

Charles winced. "Jeez, my family left me a lot of money, but it's not a bottomless pit. Eventually, the well is going to run dry. I know that's sort of a mixed metaphor, but they both have to do with holes in the ground."

"Don't worry," Stevens said, hefting one of the boxes. "We won't let you go broke. We'll do what we can until we can't, and then we'll figure out where to go from there."

After the boxes had all been delivered to the room with the boarded windows, Paul volunteered to place the books on the shelves.

"You won't get any argument from me," Greg said. "Bianca's waiting for me at home, said she's making dinner for me."

Charles laughed. "Bianca is cooking."

"It's a new thing she's trying. Even if it's inedible, I appreciate the effort."

"Come on, I'll drop you off," Charles said.

When Stevens and Paul were alone, Stevens said, "You know, it's almost nine. This can wait until tomorrow."

"I don't mind. I kind of like it better here than at my place."

It wasn't a lie. Home for Paul was a small apartment out on Gap Creek Road. A nice enough place, not a lot of room, but he didn't require a lot. However, it couldn't compare to this wonderland of books.

Stevens nodded as if he understood perfectly, which he probably did. "Just lock up on your way out."

"Of course."

Alone at last, Paul removed the sunglasses and blonde wig that were part of the disguise he wore when he and Greg went on their book-buying excursions along with the nondescript black suit and phony IDs. They paid for the books they procured from an overseas account that Bianca assured could not be traced back to them.

I'm a criminal, he thought, having no way of knowing how closely his thoughts mirrored those of his former assistant. *I'm breaking the law on a daily basis, yet I've never felt more justified in my actions.*

Paul opened the first box and inhaled the sweet

perfume of aged pages. Like wine, paper seemed to get better with age. He picked up the book on top, *The Poems of Edgar Allen Poe*, and held it just under his nose. He turned to the empty bookcase on his left and began stacking the books. This case was for new arrivals, where they stayed until they were properly catalogued, and then they were either added into the collection here or shipped out to one of the other Book Haven locations.

It took him only a half an hour to put up the books, but he didn't leave right away. He took some time to wander the room, pulling books out at random, thumbing through them, reading passages before moving on. When he reached the Ds, he stopped and stared at the spine of *Great Expectations*.

His copy, the one which had originally belonged to his great-great-grandfather, stood there amongst the rest. The one he'd been so unwilling to part with.

But here was a place he knew the book would be in good hands, a safe haven.

Removing the Dickens classic from the shelf, Paul sat down on the floor and opened the book to the first page. He could have gone out to the conference table, but he preferred to stay here, surrounded by all the worlds housed in these exquisite volumes.

The first line of *Great Expectations*, a simple declaration of how Pip came to be called by such an unusual moniker, always thrilled him. Like finding something you didn't even realize you'd lost. Falling through the portal in the pages, Paul forgot all about the world around him and entered the world of London in the mid-1800s.

Unaware that tears of joy and wonder seeped down his cheeks, Paul read deep into the night.

HUMAN BONES IN A CHINA CABINET

***Excerpt from a text conversation between
Jesse Rene Ballesteros and Mike Sifuentes:***

Mike: Hey man what you up to?

Jesse: Just bidding on some rib bones on eBay.

Jesse: Think how weird that would sound to someone
who didn't know me.

Mike: Dude I DO know you and it sounds pretty damn
weird. lol

Jesse: Everybody needs a hobby.

Mike: Yeah like restoring old cars or collecting stamps.
The animal bones were bad enough but now
human bones??? I can't believe they even sell that
shit online.

Jesse: eBay allows it as long as the bones are intended
for medical use.

Mike: But you aren't using them for any medical purposes, you're just keeping them in a china cabinet in your dining room like trophies or something. It's kind of creepy.

Jesse: So I probably shouldn't tell you that I really want a human skull to add to my collection.

Jesse: Unfortunately, the cheapest one I can find is almost 1000 dollars, way out of my price range.

Mike: 1000???? You serious????

Jesse: Yup human bones ain't cheap. Probably have to settle for a collarbone or something.

— ⸜⸝ —

Jesse frowned when the doorbell chimed. It was ten-thirty, early for a night owl like himself, but he realized rather late for the rest of the world, and he rarely got visitors, especially of the unannounced variety.

Grabbing the remote, he hit the pause button, freezing the Japanese film *Mermaid in a Manhole* just as the artist sliced into the oozing sores covering the mermaid's upper torso so he could use her pus and blood as paints. Jesse briefly considered going to his room to grab the baseball bat he kept by his bed but then laughed at his own foolishness. Life wasn't like one of the hundreds of horror movies he'd collected. It was probably just a couple of the punks that hung out at the park next to the house, entertaining themselves with a late-night game of doorbell ditch.

Leaving the den, he turned left down the short

hallway, which led to the front door. He peeked through the peephole, expecting to see an empty porch or the back of a fleeing boy; he didn't expect to see a familiar face smiling at him.

"Mike?" Jesse said, pulling the door open. "What the hell are you doing here?"

"That's no way to greet your best bud, Jesse Bear."

Jesse rolled his eyes and groaned. "I should never have told you about that childhood nickname."

"You gonna invite me in or what? I come bearing Blue Moon." Mike held up a six-pack of beer.

"You don't even drink, man."

"Yeah, but you do, and I figured you'd want to imbibe a little while we watch our movie."

"What movie?"

In his other hand, Mike held up a clear plastic CD case with a silver disc inside. "In the mood for a little *Zombie Shark*?"

"You're shitting me? That movie never got released on DVD after it aired on SyFy."

"But we live in the age of the bootleg, baby."

"Then get your ass in here, and pop that bad boy into the player."

━━⌇━━

Jesse was working on his second bottle of Blue Moon, a pleasant fog wrapping its way around his brain, while the movie played on the fifty-inch, flat-screen TV. The two men laughed and cracked jokes at the ridiculousness of the production, but that was part of its charm.

Glancing over at his friend, Jesse felt a warmth, which could only partially be attributed to the alcohol in his system, spread throughout his body. Truth was, despite texting almost every day, he and Mike typically only hung out a couple of times a year, but when they did, the camaraderie was easy and comfortable.

"So what brings a middle school teacher out so late on a weeknight?" Jesse asked, taking another swig of the beer.

Mike sipped at his water. "Well, it's Friday, which *is* technically a weeknight, but it's not like I have class to teach tomorrow or anything."

"You wouldn't rather be spending the evening with that pretty little squeeze of yours?"

"Nope, I'd rather be spending the evening with my best bud, watching a trashy B-movie and sharing some laughs like when we were growing up. I figure it's a good way for us to go out."

Something about Mike's tone sounded almost morose, and what did he mean by "a good way for us to go out"? Jesse's brain was going fuzzy around the edges, and he found it hard to concentrate, but he figured his friend was talking about his planned move to Boston, but that wasn't until the summer. They would surely get together again before then.

"Want some leftover pizza?" Jesse asked, wanting to lighten the mood. "I got about half a pepperoni still in the fridge."

He stood and was instantly assaulted by a wave of dizziness that swept over him, causing him to sway on his feet and finally plop back down on the sofa.

"Jesus, when did I become such a lightweight?" Jesse said, laughing. "Two beers and I can't even walk."

Mike didn't join in his laughter. Instead, the other

man sat down his water bottle, grimaced as if experiencing a sharp pain in his gut, then got up and walked over to the sliding glass door overlooking the backyard, where the surface of the pool glimmered in the moonlight.

"We've had a lot of good times together," he said, his voice hollow and distant, as if he were speaking from across a great chasm.

Jesse tried standing again, but this time, he toppled forward and ended up on his hands and knees. "Man, there's something not right with me."

Mike didn't answer, or if he did, Jesse didn't hear. The room seemed to pitch wildly like a ship on rough seas, and the movie, which still played on the TV, became nothing but a nonsensical jumble of piercing light and grating sound. A profound lethargy seeped into his muscles, making it hard to even lift his head to look at his friend, who still stood with his back to Jesse.

"Mike, I'm not kidding. Something's seriously wrong."

Now Mike turned to face him, the mournful expression he wore making him look twenty years older. "When you went to take a leak earlier, I spiked your beer with some ground-up sleeping pills."

Jesse glanced toward the bottle of Blue Moon with just a tiny bit of sudsy brew still at the bottom. "What? Why would you do that?"

Instead of answering, Mike walked toward him . . . then past, disappearing into the kitchen. Jesse tried to rise to his knees, but it was too much effort. He propped himself up against the sofa, his eyelids so heavy it felt as though weights hung off them, the same weights fetishists sometimes attached to their balls to stretch out their scrotums.

Jesse heard the sound of cabinets and drawers opening and slamming shut in the kitchen then a clattering from farther away. The dining room. Even with his brain not firing on full cylinders, realization dawned.

After several minutes, Mike came back into the den. He had taken a trash bag from under the kitchen sink, and it dangled from his left hand, something shifting with a sound like piccolo blocks inside. Jesse knew exactly what was in the bag without having to be told.

"Dude, you're stealing my bone collection?" he said, his words slurred, his tongue a lifeless slab of meat in his mouth.

Mike stared down at his feet, shifting the bag in his grasp so that the bones rattled again.

Jesse shook his head to clear the spots that had appeared in his vision. "All we been through, we're like brothers. Why are you doing this?"

"I do owe you an explanation," Mike said, still not looking at his so-called friend. "Do you have any idea how hard it is to live on a teacher's salary? I'm barely scraping by; I got the move coming up, and I want to ask Stephanie to marry me, but can't afford any kind of engagement ring that doesn't come in a Cracker Jack box. I don't know, when you mentioned how much human bones can go for online, it piqued my interest, and I started looking into it. At first just to satisfy my curiosity but then I started talking to some collectors with deep pockets, found a potential buyer that seemed very interested in your collection. Offered me a nice little stack of cash for it. I just couldn't resist. I'm sorry, but I couldn't."

"Did you ever think about just asking me? You think I wouldn't have helped you if I knew you were having that much trouble making ends meet?"

Mike met Jesse's eyes for the first time since returning to the den, and tears dribbled down his cheeks. "I thought I'd put enough of the pills into your beer to knock you completely out. That would have made this so much easier."

Jesse's head drooped forward so that his chin hit his chest. He forced his head back with considerable effort until it fell back against the sofa cushions. "What, you think I would have woken up and not figured out that you were the one who robbed me blind? You really think I'm that—"

He stopped speaking when Mike raised his right hand, revealing the gleaming butcher knife that had also come from the kitchen.

"I thought collecting human bones was creepy," Mike said, staring down at the knife as if contemplating his reflection in the blade, "but the buyer I've been in contact with has an even creepier hobby. He collects human organs."

Jesse tried to crawl away, get to his cell, but his limbs had gone numb, and he could only sit propped against the sofa, slowly sliding to the right.

Mike held the knife out in front of him and slowly approached his friend, his stride reluctant but steady. "What he's paying me for these bones is nothing compared to what he'll give me for a fresh heart."

WELCOME HOME

EVAN AWOKE ALONE in the bed. As usual.

He'd tried to explain to Steve that one of the perks of having nowhere to be and no responsibilities was how one could sleep in as late as they wanted. Still, Steve was up before the sun most mornings.

Stretching languidly, Evan threw back the covers and padded to the restroom. After finishing his business, he made his way downstairs in only a pair of too-tight boxer-briefs to find Steve in his typical spot.

Sitting in the armchair by the front window, scribbling away in a spiral-bound notebook.

"Unbelievable," Evan said, grinning. "All these years, and you're still keeping those journals."

Steve glanced up and snorted a laugh. "Just like the food that mysteriously appears in the cupboards and fridge every morning, these notebooks keep appearing. Might as well fill them up. Besides, you're one to talk. All these years, and you're still running around like a go-go dancer. You do know there are several of these in the closet upstairs, right?" He held out his arms to indicate the oversized robe that swaddled him like a cocoon.

"What's it matter?" Evan said, doing a little twirl in front of Steve. "There's no one here but the two of us, and you've seen me in less."

A blush crept into Steve's checks, and he averted his stare back to the notebook.

"You're so sexy when you get all shy and embarrassed," Evan said, bending to place his hands on the chair's arms and leaning in for a kiss. At first, Steve's lips were tight and unresponsive, but then he opened his mouth and gave in. "How about I make us some breakfast?" Evan said as he pulled back. "Scrambled eggs and bacon?"

"Sounds good. Need some help?"

"No, you finish your opus. If we ever get out of this house, those that come after us might find it an interesting read."

One more kiss, then Evan headed toward the kitchen.

Steve watched the young man disappear through the swinging door into the kitchen then returned his attention to the notebook in his lap. His stomach cramped with a mixture of guilt, confusion, frustration, anger, but also love, hope, contentment, complacency. He dealt with this churning gumbo of emotion the only way he knew how. He wrote.

I think it has been about a year since my relationship with Evan turned sexual, and I'm still not entirely comfortable with it. Every morning, I get up and tell myself I'm going to put an end to it, but then he looks into my eyes, and I melt. Just like a character in some cheesy romance novel. When we're together, it just feels right, but it can't be . . . can it? I've known him since he was twelve; I practically raised him like a father. That's why this feels so incestuous. Yet I'm not his father, and he's not twelve years old anymore. We've been trapped in this house together for ten years, at least, though I haven't been consistently keeping track of the days for a while. Evan has to be somewhere in his early 20s by now, a consenting adult. And the truth is, he was the one who made the first move, the one who'd seduced me. I admit I had been feeling an attraction to him before then, but I doubt I'd have ever worked up the nerve to act on it, and I resisted Evan's advances at first, but I'm only human. Some might call it loneliness and convenience. Being trapped inside this house with no contact with anyone else, maybe we just clung to one another because we are all we've got. But it's more than that too: I love him. I think I've loved him from the moment he showed up on the doorstep of this damn house. Not in a romantic way, not back then, but I still loved him, and that was why I couldn't leave him alone here even though I had a brief window to be free. That window is closed now. Five or so years ago, I tried to leave and found the invisible barrier was back in place, keeping me locked inside. I wasn't going to leave him alone; I swear I wasn't. I had this notion that I could save him. Since the rules of this place seem to be that once inside you can't leave unless someone else shows up and enters the house of their own free will, I thought maybe if I got outside and then reentered the house, maybe then Evan would be able to leave. However, the barrier was back in place, and

I wasn't able to try my little experiment. Maybe it would have worked if I'd done it as soon as he'd first come into this house all those years ago, but I had been so stunned by Al's lack of concern over the fate of a child being left here alone, his abandonment of me as he seized his chance and walked away without even looking back, that I didn't even think of such a thing. I just knew I had to stay and take care of the boy. The boy who is now a man, who shares a bed with me, who has become my lover. As right as it feels, it also feels wrong. But everything about this situation feels wrong, so could this be the one instance where two wrongs really do make a right?

Steve put down the pen and closed the notebook. Pouring out his feelings and thoughts onto the page didn't quiet the rumblings inside, but it did quell them somewhat. Putting the book aside, he stood up and went to help Evan with breakfast.

–◝◜–

Later that afternoon, as they sat in the living room playing Go Fish with a worn-out deck of cards, someone knocked on the door.

The two men froze, Steve with his hand reached out to place three 7s on the coffee table. Their eyes locked, but neither of them moved nor breathed. Steve would have probably thought it was an auditory hallucination, only Evan seemed to have heard it too.

A moment later, the knock came again.

"Oh my God, it's really happening," Evan said in a hoarse voice. "Part of me never believed it really would; I thought we'd die in this house, but it's finally happening."

"Calm down," Steve said, but his heart beat so hard he feared it might burst from his chest like the creature in the movie *Alien*. "Whoever it is, we don't want to scare them away by acting like complete freaks. We need to act normal. As normal as possible under the circumstances. Run upstairs, and get dressed."

Evan looked down at himself. While Steve had changed into some sweats just after breakfast, Evan was still wearing only his underwear. There was a dazed, stunned look in his eyes, and Steve had to snap his fingers in front of the young man's face several times to get him to focus.

"Go put on some clothes," he said, speaking slowly. "Don't be long though."

Evan nodded but still did not move. Only when the knock at the door came again did his paralysis break, and he bolted from the room and up the staircase.

Steve stood on wobbly legs and headed into the

foyer. He felt lightheaded, like his brains had been scooped out and replaced with cotton candy. Evan had said part of him had never believed this day would come, that someone would show up at the door offering the prospect of freedom, and Steve had to admit he hadn't believed it either. He'd suspected he would live out the rest of his life in this house with Evan, and if he were brutally honest, he'd made peace with that.

Approaching the door, he found a single thought repeating on a loop in his mind: *please don't be another child, please don't be another child, please don't be another child . . .*

Gripping the doorknob, Steve wrenched open the door and almost laughed when he saw the person standing outside.

Not a child—quite the opposite. An old man, stooped and emaciated, leaning heavily on a wooden cane while clutching a sheaf of papers in his free hand. He'd half-turned from the door, perhaps preparing to leave but turned back to stare at Steve with pale eyes.

"Can I help you?" Steve said, hearing the nervous whine in the words.

The old man continued to stare then lifted his gaze to take in the front of the house. "You know, I've canvassed this neighborhood more times than I could count in the last decade, but I don't think I've ever stopped here. I'm not even sure I ever noticed this house before."

"It has that blending-in effect. You said you were canvassing? Is this for a political candidate . . . ?" Steve let his words trail off, as he had no idea if they were anywhere near an election, and even if so, he had no way of knowing any candidates by name.

"Nothing like that," the man said, rustling the papers in his left hand. "I'm handing out these flyers, looking for my son."

The old man held out the stack of papers, and Steve took one off the top, knowing what he was going to see even before glancing down at it.

At the top was a black and white picture of Evan as he'd looked when Steve first met him, an open-faced boy with a big smile, dressed in his Little League uniform. The bottom of the page was taken up by an artist's projection of what Evan might look like today. Close but not quite accurate. The nose and hair were all wrong. In between the pictures, in block text, was this message: EVAN ROBERT THOMPSON MISSING SINCE JULY 12 2006.

Steve felt cold all over, and his breath rasped from his lungs with the sound of air escaping a slashed tire. Behind him, he was distantly aware of the sound of footsteps clomping down the stairs, and then Evan was next to him.

"So, who do we have—"

Evan's words cut off abruptly when his gaze found the flyer in Steve's hands.

"Evan?" said the man in the doorway, squinting at the young man standing next to Steve. "Evan, is that you? Is that my boy?"

Evan clutched at Steve's arm, his grip like a clamp. "Daddy?"

⁓⫶⁓

The old man on the doorstep didn't look exactly like the man Evan remembered from his childhood. He remembered his father as hale and strong, with a thick head of hair and bright eyes that twinkled with humor. The man before him now was a wasted husk, thin as a rope with receding hair more gray than black. His eyes were flat and empty. He looked like he'd aged far more than the ten years since Evan had last seen his father. Certain things about the man, the shape of his mouth and the downturn of the nose, were familiar though. Beyond those superficial familiarities, however, there was some indefinable quality, an aura about the man, and Evan simply *knew*.

"Daddy," he said again, his voice barely a whisper.

Tears dribbled down the old man's cheeks, and the papers he held fluttered to the ground. "Evan, my sweet Evan, I can't believe this. I've been looking for you for so long; I've passed flyers around in this neighborhood probably hundreds of times because this was where you had gone to sell those stupid candy bars. Everyone said I was crazy to still be looking after all this time, the police shut the case long ago, but I knew you were out here somewhere. I just knew if I—"

"Stop!" Evan shouted. His father had raised a foot to step across the threshold, but now he backed up quickly, startled no doubt by the vehemence in Evan's voice.

"What's wrong? What did I do?"

"You can't come in," Evan said then turned an imploring gaze to Steve. "We can't let him come in; we just can't. He's my dad."

Steve nodded, and in his eyes, Evan saw all the compassion and tenderness he'd first fallen in love with. There were worse fates than being trapped for the rest of your life with this man.

"I don't understand what's going on," his father said and took a step forward again.

"No!" Evan threw himself at the doorway, striking the invisible barrier and rebounding, falling into Steve's arms.

This brought his father to a halt again, his brow furrowed with consternation. "What's happening? Evan, talk to me."

"I will, just stay outside. I'm going to explain, but I need you to stay where you are."

His father eyed Steve suspiciously. "Is this man holding you against your will?"

"No. Dad, I'll tell you everything, just promise you won't come inside."

The man hesitated then nodded.

Evan hesitated as well. How was he supposed to explain this to his father? He barely understood it himself, had come to accept the mystery over the years. How could he put it into words?

"This house, it's some kind of . . . I don't know, cosmic roach motel. You can check in, but you can't check out. At least not until someone else checks in. I came knocking on the door here and walked inside with my box of chocolates, and then I couldn't leave again. I don't know what causes it, but when a person enters the house, some kind of barrier goes up, sealing them inside. The barrier only drops if someone else enters the house to take their place."

His father didn't respond for several moments, just stared at him, his expression unreadable. Evan was sure the man thought him insane. It sounded insane.

"So," his father said at last, "you're saying you've been trapped in this house ever since you disappeared, but that if I were to walk through the door, you'd finally be able to leave?"

"Yes, but then you would be trapped inside."

"It's true, Mr. Thompson," Steve said, then he placed his hands against the barrier and leaned all his weight against it, cords popping up on his neck from the strain as he pushed against what seemed to be thin air.

"If my son walked through the door, why weren't you able to leave?"

"There was someone else here with me back then. He left; I chose to stay."

"Steve took care of me," Evan said.

"Who's that on the staircase?"

Both Evan and Steve whirled around. The staircase was empty. When Evan turned back to the doorway, his father was standing inside it.

"Jesus, what have you done?" Evan said, feeling something twist inside him.

Instead of answering, his father turned back to the door and reached out a hand. It flattened against the barrier. "It's really true," he said in a quiet, wondering voice.

"You should have listened to me," Evan said but threw himself in his father's arms. The two embraced though his father's grip was weak.

"Get out of here," he rasped in Evan's ear. "Both of you, while you still can."

"Dad, I can't leave you here."

"You have to; it's what I want. Besides, I won't be here for long."

"What do you mean?"

His father took a deep breath, smiled sadly, and said, "I'm dying. I have cancer, started in my prostate, but by the time they caught it, it had spread all over.

Metastasized. Nothing they can do for it, not even chemo. Doctors say I have a month, two at the most. I decided to use my last breath to keep looking for you."

"Where's Mom?"

His father looked at his feet and shook his head. "She's gone. Committed suicide a year after you went missing. She couldn't live with the loss."

Evan's emotions were huge and complex. Years ago he'd given up the notion of ever being reunited with his parents, but now, old wounds were open afresh as he found out one parent was dead and the other was dying.

His father took his hand and squeezed it. "This is why I found you after all these years, to give this gift to you. It doesn't matter if I'm stuck in this house; I'll be dead before the seasons change anyway. But my last act can be to finally free you."

Steve put a hand on his shoulder. "Evan, I know this is hard for you, but your father is right. If we're going to go, we have to do it now. We have no idea how long we'll be able to pass through the door before the barrier goes up again."

Evan began to cry, deep and painful sobs that wracked his body. He hugged his father fiercely, clinging to him like a life preserver. His father returned the embrace for a bit then gently pushed him away. "Go now, please. I love you, my boy."

"I love you too, Dad."

Still weeping, the tears nearly blinding him, Evan took Steve's hand, and they stepped over the threshold.

—✴︎—

Steve stood on the edge of the property, his head thrown back. It had been so long since he'd been outside, felt the breeze on his skin, felt the sun beating down on his face. He knew Evan was hurting, but he couldn't keep a grin off his face. *Freedom.* Before his car had broken down outside this house, it had been only a word to him, an abstract concept, but now he truly understood it.

"Look at the house," Evan said from behind him.

Steve turned and glanced at the house. It seemed so small and unassuming, blending in with the trees and shrubbery. As he looked, it seemed to blend in even more.

Camouflage, he thought. People probably passed by this house every day, and it was virtually invisible to them.

Evan held a hand over his eyes to shield them from the sun, staring intently at the front windows. "Do you think my dad is still watching? I can't see him."

Steve stepped up behind Evan and wrapped his arms around the younger man's waist. "He could be standing in the doorway, and we probably can't see him. I think the house prevents it."

Evan turned around and kissed Steve with passion and fire, and then he buried his face in Steve's chest. Steve held him as he cried.

Finally, after taking a few shaky breaths, Evan pulled back slightly and looked up at Steve. "So, what do we do now? Where do we go?"

"I don't know," Steve said, his grin returning. "But it's kind of exciting, isn't it?"

The two men joined hands, kissed again, and then began walking down the street, leaving the house behind.

C U SOON

MONICA WAS BURIED with her cell phone.

No one thought it strange. She'd loved her iPhone with its pink case and the silver spangles all over it, always had it clutched in her hand texting, Facebooking, Tweeting, Instagramming, playing any number of games. It seemed only natural she be buried with the phone.

The only one who thought it grotesque was Monica's boyfriend, Philip, but then he was the only one who knew her phone had killed her.

⚬⚬⚬

Actually, *he* had killed her, or so he thought at the funeral as he stared down at her in the coffin, the phone resting on her chest with her hands folded over it.

I did this to her. Because I couldn't wait fifteen minutes until she got to my house to talk to her, because I had to keep texting, because I was distracting her.

Philip hadn't told anyone he and Monica had been texting when she lost control of her car and drove it into the ravine. Her last message to him was "C U soon", apparently sent just seconds before the crash.

Perhaps his return message had surprised her, causing her to involuntarily jerk the wheel or something. He meant it only as a joke, a tease, something to turn her on. He'd never texted a dick pic before, but he thought it might excite her.

Instead, it got her killed.

You don't know that; you don't even know if she got the picture before the crash. Even if you hadn't been texting her, you know she would have been on the phone doing something. A new Facebook update, a funny tweet, scrolling through YouTube videos.

In his heart, he still felt responsible, and he knew others would think he was responsible too, which was why he hadn't told anyone about the texting or the picture. Monica's parents said her phone had been damaged beyond repair in the accident, evidenced by the shattered screen on display in the coffin, and Philip had deleted everything off his own phone. He didn't want anyone to know.

He knew though, and as he stood by the graveside, he wondered how he was going to live with the knowledge.

―᠕᠊―

"Philip."

He paused at the sound of his name. He considered not turning around, pretending he hadn't heard, getting into his car, and driving away.

"Philip, do you have a minute?"

Taking a deep, steeling breath, Philip finally turned to face Monica's parents.

They stood close together, leaning on one another as if neither had the strength to stand without the support of the other. They seemed to have aged twenty years since Monica's death, Mr. Dew's hair streaked with more gray and the lines around Mrs. Dew's mouth etched so deep they looked like trenches.

Philip wasn't sure what to say to them. What did you say to parents whose seventeen-year-old daughter, their only child, was dead? Especially when you felt you may be to blame for her death? He stood in silence, staring at them as they stared at him.

Finally, Mr. Dew cleared his throat and said, "We were just wondering, would you like to come back to the house?"

"Um, I thought the gathering at your place was just for the immediate family."

A weak smile flickered at the corners of Mrs. Dew's mouth, making her countenance somehow even more tragic. "You and Monica were a couple since you were fourteen. I know you loved her, and she loved you. You're like family."

Philip grimaced as if in the grips of painful cramps. Tendrils of guilt and shame wrapped around him like a family of anacondas squeezing the life from his body. He looked back at his parents, who'd come separately in the Volvo; they waited by the car, looking somber themselves. They'd known Monica for years and probably thought of her as extended family the way Mr. and Mrs. Dew thought of him. Seemed everyone was suffering . . .

. . . *and it's all my fault.*

"I . . . I think I just want to be alone," Philip stammered.

Mrs. Dew nodded. "I understand, but I want you to know you're welcome at our house anytime."

Mr. Dew held out a hand to shake, but he ended up pulling Philip into a tight hug. When he finally let go, Mrs. Dew enfolded him in a hug of her own. It was almost too much to bear, and Philip felt like screaming, confessing, but instead, he just scurried away to his car. He spoke briefly with his parents, telling them he wanted to drive around for a while before heading home.

He had no destination in mind and coasted around town, avoiding Miller Road, the site of Monica's accident. There was a cross marking the spot where she'd run into the ravine, and he didn't want to see it. Didn't even want to think about it.

Not that he could think about anything else.

After half an hour, he found himself at the park on Belmont Avenue. A gaggle of children swarmed over the playground equipment with their parents sitting on the benches nearby, but Philip managed to find a quiet spot at a picnic table under a large Maple by the gurgling fountain.

He sat on top of the table, wishing he could will his mind to go blank. If he walked over to the tree and started banging his head against the trunk, could he induce amnesia? He craved a blank slate, tabula rasa.

Seeking a distraction, Philip glanced over to the closest jungle gym, watching the children climbing all over it, laughing and shrieking with delight. Such innocence emanated from them, a sense of the pure hope that only comes from ignorance. They knew nothing about the harshness of the world, the depth of pain a soul could endure, the incapacitating breadth of guilt.

They didn't know what it felt like to kill your girlfriend.

C U SOON

In his pocket, his phone vibrated, indicating a text message. Figuring it would be his parents checking on him, he pulled out the phone and pulled up the message.

"Miss U"

Philip gasped and nearly dropped the phone, a chill engulfing his body as if he'd been dunked in a vat of ice water. The world around him faded out until he existed in a gray vacuum where even he felt insubstantial, the only thing of substance the phone in his hand.

It wasn't the message itself that caused this reaction but the sender.

Monica.

~⋅\⋅/⋅~

Philip returned home and went straight to his room. He didn't tell his parents about the text; he didn't plan to tell *anyone* about the text. It was impossible.

The truth of it stared back at him as he sat on his bed, staring down at the message. "Miss U."

Her name, her number.

But it couldn't be from Monica; of course he knew that. Someone was playing a cruel and heartless joke on him. Who would do such a thing?

How could it be someone else? This was Monica's cell number; it even displayed a little picture of her next to her name.

Her cell phone was busted and buried with her though. He'd seen it. Unless she was texting from the grave . . .

He jumped when the phone buzzed in his hand. A new text message, again from Monica's number.

"Its lonely here an dark"

Tears spilled down Philip's cheeks, and his chest felt tight, like a large weight was crushing him, making it hard to breathe. Monica had always left out apostrophes in her text messages, often used "an" instead of "and", and rarely used closing punctuation. If this was someone playing a prank, they were going to great pains to make it authentic.

"Who is this?" he texted back.

"Your kitten"

With a strangled cry, Philip tossed the phone from him. It landed on the edge of the bed.

Kitten . . . his secret nickname for Monica. He'd started calling her that just after the first time they'd slept together. As in "sex kitten". They only used the nickname in private. He'd never mentioned it to his closest friends, and as far as he knew, neither had Monica, although he couldn't be certain.

He couldn't be sure of anything right now.

His mind on overload and in danger of a meltdown, he curled up on the bed and cried himself to sleep, praying to a God he wasn't sure existed that he'd wake up to find the last few days had been nothing but a nightmare.

~·—

Philip awoke to the sound of his mother's voice. She sat next to him on the bed, shaking his shoulder gently. He was denied even the moment of blissful amnesia that often comes when waking up. The truth of what happened to Monica crashed back onto him as soon as his eyes opened. Even his dreams had been haunted by her, though all that remained was a tattered image of her sitting on top of the jungle gym at the Belmont Avenue park, perched on the highest bar while texting furiously on her cell. He had called to her, but she hadn't looked up, as if she couldn't even hear him.

The dream was quickly dissipating, leaving behind a reality far worse, and his mother smiled down at him with an even more painful sympathy.

"You've been asleep for hours," she said.

Philip glanced at the window to see it was full dark outside. The only light in the room came from the hall, a yellow block falling onto the carpet like a wedge of cheese.

"I've got supper ready."

"Mom, I don't have much of an appetite," Philip said, wiping away the gritty gunk from the corners of his eyes.

His mother reached out and gripped his arm. "You haven't eaten anything all day. You really need to try to get some food in your stomach."

Philip pushed himself up, leaning his back against the headboard. "I just don't think I could keep anything down."

She nodded, a few tears making slug trails down her cheeks. Her voice cracked when she spoke. "I know this is a rough time. For everybody. Monica was a special girl, and her death has left a hole in all of us, a wound only time will heal."

Philip hated it when his mother talked like one of the inspirational books she always read, but he swallowed the sarcastic retort rising to his lips. She meant well and was just doling out a little comfort. There were worse crimes. He should know.

"Maybe later," he said. "After I get a bath."

"Okay, sweetie. I'll put your plate in the oven."

On her way out, his mother turned on the floor lamp by the closet. Philip stayed where he was for a few moments, his knees pulled up to his chest. His phone was no longer on the edge of the mattress. He assumed it must have slid off sometime while he slept, landing on the carpeted floor on the far side of the bed. He cringed and scooted farther toward the other side as if a venomous snake would leap up and strike.

Perhaps it was all in my head. The funeral, the guilt, maybe it was too much stress, and I hallucinated the texts.

Philip didn't know what it said about his mental state that being delusional was the preferable choice, but it couldn't be a good sign.

Finally breaking the paralysis keeping him frozen, he crawled across the mattress, which suddenly seemed as large as Texas despite only being a twin, and peered over the side. The phone lay screen down, just an innocuous hunk of plastic, glass, and circuits . . . yet the sight of it filled him with a childish dread.

With a trembling hand, he reached down and grabbed the phone. It felt hot to the touch, probably just a psychosomatic response. He held it in his lap before flipping it over.

He had twenty missed texts, all from Monica. He deleted them without reading a single one.

~•~

Returning to school was weird.

Monica had always been a popular girl, and her absence shrouded East Hampton High School in dusty spider webs of stunned grief. Students shuffled along the halls like zombies, the old-fashioned Romero kind, eyes vacant and their movements sluggish. Even those who hadn't known Monica personally seemed affected, as if the very knowledge that someone their own age could meet with such a tragic end fundamentally destroyed their worldview. Their first taste of mortality.

On top of the funereal atmosphere, Philip had to deal with everyone giving him pitying looks of sympathy, what he was coming to think of as the *poor little you* look. Not just from other students but also teachers, cafeteria workers, even the old Mexican janitor. Mrs. Clifford, the school guidance counselor, stopped him in the hall after third period and asked if he wanted to come back to her office and talk. After politely declining, he scurried away.

He didn't want to talk. Not to Mrs. Clifford, not to his friends, not to his parents, not to anyone. He would have stayed out of school if his parents hadn't insisted on him gettng back to his normal routine.

As if anything could ever be normal again.

At lunch, he didn't eat. He went out to the quad and sat by himself under the flagpole. Several of his friends tried to talk to him, but his curt responses and icy stares sent them packing. He knew they meant well, but their suffocating sympathy was more than he could take at the moment.

His phone buzzed in his pocket, and even before looking at the screen, he knew it wasn't going to be one of his buddies, or his Mom, or even a wrong number.

It could only be Monica.

"Y wont U talk 2 me"

Philip felt tears sliding down his cheeks, and he

squeezed the phone in his hands, barely resisting the temptation to hurl it away from him and watch it explode against the pavement. He began jabbing his fingers at the touchscreen keyboard, banging out a reply.

"Please leave me alone."

The response was almost immediate. "Dont U love me anymore"

"Who is this?"

"Your kitten"

"Stop it! Why are you doing this to me?"

"I love U and miss U"

Philip turned the cell phone off and stuffed it back in his pocket. The tears stung his eyes, but he didn't wipe them away.

Standing, he moved back toward the building. He considered going to the principal's office and telling Mr. Sanders about the texts. Maybe they could get the authorities involved, find out who was sending the messages and how they were using Monica's number.

Only, instead of going to Mr. Sanders' office, Philip went to the restroom and locked himself in the handicapped stall. He knew he should tell someone, but he couldn't bring himself to do it.

Like with the stinging tears, on some level he felt he deserved this pain. It was his punishment.

～◀✦↙～

Philip didn't turn his phone back on until after supper. His mother had made meatloaf, his favorite, but he barely touched it. Mostly just moved the food around on his plate with the fork. His father had asked him about school, trying so desperately to act like everything was normal. It made Philip want to scream.

After twenty minutes of torture, he asked to be excused from the table and retreated to his room. He took out his phone and laid it on the coverlet in front of him, staring down at the black screen. He reached for it a few times but drew his hand back before his finger brushed the case.

He turned on the television, tuning into some mindless reality show about horrible people doing horrible things and feeling good about it, hoping to distract himself from thoughts of Monica. Yet he couldn't concentrate on the show, which seemed to be about a group of "friends" who spent all their time backstabbing one another; his eyes kept straying to the phone like lead shavings drawn to a magnet.

The television providing no solace, he grabbed his iPad and got online. Facebook proved to be nothing but glass in his wounds, his wall filled with words of sympathy and remembrances of Monica. He pulled up the music on the tablet, but every song reminded him of her.

Finally he gave up, grabbed the phone and turned it on. He expected to find a dozen or so message waiting, but there was only one.

"I don't blame U"

—⫶—

The texts came regularly over the next few days. Philip didn't respond to any of them, but he read every single one. Mostly messages about how lonely she was, how much she missed him, how what happened wasn't his fault. Maybe whoever was doing this wasn't trying to punish Philip but comfort him.

How could anyone know the secrets he shared only with Monica? The texts also sounded so much like her.

Lying on his bed at half past midnight, he stared at the latest text—"I wish U were lyin next 2 me"—and mumbled to himself, "This is crazy."

Which was the unvarnished truth. What was he considering here? That Monica's ghost was communicating with him via text? It *was* Monica's phone number, and he knew her cell was buried under six feet of dirt and rock with her body.

Philip didn't know what he believed. All he knew for certain was that the messages were starting to be more balm than barb. Taking a deep breath, he typed.

"I wish you were here next to me too."

Tears trailed down his cheeks when he read the response.

"Luv U"

"I love you too," he whispered then drifted off to sleep cradling the phone to his chest.

⁓⁓⁓

After that, Philip stopped doubting. In church, Reverend Phelps always talked about miracles; why couldn't this be one? Maybe miracles weren't just for saints and holy men. Perhaps even sinners could feel the hand of God. He had been taught to believe death wasn't the end. This could be the proof.

Or possibly he was just insane. The idea didn't disturb him as much as he might have expected, not as long as it resulted in this tenuous connection to Monica.

She continued to text, and he continued answering. He withdrew from his friends, his parents, spending all his time shut up in his room. All his meals were taken in his room as well, much to his mother's dismay. His thumbs had developed calluses from the nearly constant texting. His whole world had shrunk down to just the screen of his cell phone, waiting for the next message.

One evening, two months after Monica's death, Philip's dad knocked on his bedroom door. Philip sent the text he'd just written and then turned the phone face-down on his lap.

"Messaging with your friends?" his dad asked, rocking on the balls of his feet with his hands stuffed into his pockets. The very picture of discomfort.

"Just watching YouTube videos."

His dad looked over at the plate of food on the nightstand—spaghetti with meatballs. "You barely touched your supper."

Philip shrugged. "I'm not all that hungry tonight."

Looking back toward the doorway as if he wanted to be anywhere but here, his dad sighed before he walked forward and took a seat on the edge of the bed. Philip, attempting to make the move seem casual, tucked his phone under his pillow.

"Son, are you all right? Well, that's a stupid question; of course you're not all right, but it's not healthy for you to isolate this way."

"I just need some time," Philip said. "A little time alone to sort things out."

"I understand that, but you can take that too far. Your mom and I are always here if you need to talk. If you're not comfortable coming to us, go to some of your friends. If not that, we could always find someone for you to talk to."

"A shrink?"

"A counselor. There's no shame in it. We all need help sometimes."

"I'm fine, Dad. I don't need to talk to anyone."

Except Monica, he thought, his fingers itching to type out a new text to her.

His dad nodded, lingered on the bed for a moment more, then finally stood. "Well, you know we're here for you if you need . . . anything."

"Thanks, I'll remember."

His dad looked like he still had more he wanted to say, but in the end, he took the plate of uneaten pasta and left the room.

As soon as the door closed, Philip snatched the phone from under the pillow.

—◦◦◦—

A week later, he found himself standing on the sidewalk outside of a house he never expected to visit again.

Monica's house.

It was a simple, single-story, Ranch-style home of red brick. Philip had always thought the place rather nondescript, but now, a sinister air seemed to hang over it like angry, blue-black storm clouds. Perhaps he only felt that way because of the lawn's condition.

Mr. Dew had always taken such pride in keeping the yard neat and landscaped, but now, long-browned grass rustled in the breeze with the sound of conspirators whispering.

Philip seriously considered getting back in his car and driving away, but he'd made a promise to Monica. She'd asked him to check on her folks; she wanted to know they were okay.

"Why can't you contact them the way you do me?" he'd asked her in a text.

"Idk mayb because we were textin when I died it bonded us somehow I just know I need U to check on them for me"

"I feel funny being around them."

"Please Phil do it 4 your kitten I just need to know how their doing"

So here he was. He owed it to her after everything that had happened. Steeling himself with a deep breath, he walked across the jungle the lawn had become, stepping up onto the front stoop. He rang the bell and waited. After a full minute passed with no response, he rang the bell again and followed it up by knocking. As much as he didn't want to be here, he wanted to get this over with. He wasn't sure he'd be able to work up the nerve to try again.

Another minute and still no answer. Both Mr. and Mrs. Dew's cars were in the driveway, and he could hear the faint sound of a TV playing somewhere inside the house. He knocked again, louder this time, and called out, "Hello, is anybody home?"

He had just pulled out his cell to call the Dews' number when he heard footsteps shuffling inside. The door opened a crack, and Mr. Dew stood there in a frayed blue bathrobe, his hair sticking up in wild tufts and corkscrews, his usually clean-shaven face covered in a tangle of unkempt beard. His bleary stare made it seem as if he didn't recognize Philip on his doorstep, but then he blinked rapidly, shook his head, and said, "Oh, hey Phil. What are you doing here?"

"Um, you said I could stop by and visit anytime."

"Yeah, that's right. Well, come on in. Do mind the mess."

Mess was an understatement. Philip actually had

to stifle a gasp as he entered the gloomy living room. Garbage covered every surface, even large portions of the floor. Fast food containers, pizza boxes, soiled paper towels, soda and beer cans, dirty dishes. The putrid stench of sewers and landfills burned in Philip's nostrils. In the far corner of the room, a TV glowed, providing the only light. On an armchair across from the TV was what Philip at first mistook for a pile of dirty laundry. He did gasp when the laundry shifted, leaning further into the light.

Mrs. Dew, all curled up under a fuzzy blanket, her face marked with smeared makeup that seemed like it may have been applied several weeks earlier. She glanced in Philip's direction but then returned her dead-eyed gaze back to the TV without speaking. On the screen, a shaky, slightly out-of-focus scene played out of a woman in a rocking chair holding a baby. At first, Philip thought it was one of those found footage films that were all the rage . . .

Until he recognized the woman as a young Mrs. Dew.

"Old home movies," Mr. Dew said as he sat heavily on the sofa, heedless of the fact that he crushed a potato chip bag in the process. "Our little Monica was only two months old there. We also have some footage of her first dance recital and the Christmas play in sixth grade, where she was the lead elf. Want to sit down and watch with us?"

Philip glanced back at the TV, seeing a youthful Mr. Dew holding the baby and making funny faces, and shook his head. "I can't stay long."

"At least have a bite to eat." Mr. Dew flipped open a pizza box on the cushion next to him, unfazed by cockroaches as big as fun-sized candy bars crawling all over the few shriveled slices left inside.

"Thanks, but I've already eaten. I just wanted to stop by and check on you guys, see how you've been doing."

"We're doing okay," Mr. Dew said despite the evidence to the contrary. "I won't lie; it's been rough, but life goes on, or so they say."

"I think the secret is getting back into a routine," Philip said as if he had any idea what he was talking about, just repeating the empty words his parents had offered to him. "How's work going?"

"Ah, we haven't been back since the funeral. The plant is being pretty understanding with me, but the bank let Judith go."

"Mrs. Dew, you lost your job at the bank?"

The woman didn't answer, didn't even seem aware that anyone else was in the room. She remained frozen, eyes glued to the TV screen.

Mr. Dew answered for her. "Yeah, those bitches pretended to be all sympathetic at the funeral, showing up after with casseroles and cakes, but when Judith wasn't back at work in a week's time, they cut her loose. Fucking cunts!"

Philip had never heard Mr. Dew use that kind of language before, and it temporarily stunned him speechless. He watched in horror as Mr. Dew picked up a slice of pizza, shook off a cockroach, then took a bite.

"Well, I really need to get going," Philip said, already backing toward the door.

"Thanks for stopping by, and don't be a stranger, Champ. Remember, you're family."

"Yeah, sure thing. Bye, Mrs. Dew."

Again, no response. He wouldn't even have been sure she was alive if she didn't blink slowly every few seconds. As if she were in some kind of waking catatonia. Mr. Dew waved as Philip hurried out the door, cutting across the lawn. By the time he made it to his car, his cell was already buzzing in his pocket.

"How R they"

∼⋰⋰∼

The night was quiet, the sky clear and shimmering with tiny pinpricks of light. A quarter moon hung low, shedding a frosty glow over the cemetery.

Philip reclined on his back in the grass, right next to Monica's grave. Tears slid down either side of his face to dampen the grass like morning dew. The tombstone had been freshly placed, a large marble slab, and the grave itself already sprouted new growth to cover over the dirt weighing down on the girl's coffin.

Philip sent a new text.

"I'm so sorry."

"It just kills me 2 know my folks R sufferin or it would if i was still livin"

"It's my fault, I caused all this."

"Bein stuck here all alone is bad enuf now knowin this its just 2 much"

Philip wanted so badly for Monica to tell him again that this wasn't his fault; he craved absolution. But why should she absolve him? This *was* all his fault. He was not only responsible for Monica's death but he had ruined her parents' lives. He didn't deserve forgiveness, not after all the pain he'd caused. Was still causing.

As if to drive the point home, he received another text from Monica.

"Im so lonely id rather be N hell than stuck N this limbo all alone"

"I'm here for you. Always."

"Its not enuf i luv u but its not enuf"

Philip hesitated, his fingers trembling as he contemplated sending the message he'd been working up the nerve to send for the past hour. Finally, he took a deep breath and started tapping at the screen.

"Maybe we can be together again."

"Wat R U talkin about"

"I can't live with the guilt of what I've done to you and your parents."

"U cant be serious"

"I am, I've thought a lot about this, and I want to be with you. No matter what."

"R U sure?"

"If you'll have me."

"O yes I miss U so much"

"Then I'm ready."

"Wat R people gonna think when they see all these messages"

"Nothing, I'm going to delete them."

"I luv U an will C U soon"

"I love you too," Philip whispered and then deleted the string of text messages between himself and Monica. In his hands, the phone began to vibrate again, and he saw his mother was calling. No doubt worried and wondering where he was so late. He turned the phone off and tossed it aside.

He crawled onto the top of Monica's grave with his back up against the tombstone, reaching into the pocket of his jeans to pull out the penknife his grandfather had given him for his thirteenth birthday. A cheap thing, but it was the last thing his grandfather had given him before he died, so Philip carried it with him always. He flicked it open and stared down at the blade. Traditionally a razor was used for such things, but the point was sharp and should do quite nicely.

He closed his eyes then sliced into his right wrist.

— ⚡ —

Mr. and Mrs. Dew returned home after Philip's funeral, Judith in her smartest black dress and Roger in his best suit. Trash still filled the living room but not as much as before. They were in the process of getting everything cleaned up again.

Judith sat down on the recliner, her purse resting on her lap like a small child. "I didn't expect it to be so quick," she said.

Roger remained standing by the front door. "Neither did I, but it's what we wanted."

Digging through her purse, Judith brought out the iPhone in its pink case with the silver spangles all over it. "I guess we should destroy this now. I mean, it was supposed to have been buried with her after all."

"Yeah."

"Do you think anyone suspects it was an old cell we smashed and put in an identical case in her coffin?"

"Why would they?"

"I guess you're right," she said, staring down at her daughter's phone. "You know, I wanted him to suffer, but I thought he'd eventually crack and just confess the part he played in our Monica's death. I didn't really think he'd go all the way and kill himself, not really.

Even when he was texting about doing it, I didn't really think he'd go through with it."

Roger walked over and gently removed the phone from his wife's hands. "What's done is done. I'm going to take this down to the basement and pulverize it with the hammer, then I'll bury the pieces in the backyard."

After her husband left the room, Judith remained in the chair for a few moments. She had expected to feel some sense of vindication or satisfaction, but instead, there was only emptiness inside.

Finally, she got up and started gathering more trash.

END OF THE WORLD
BENEDICTION

They sat in silence in the stands,
Awaiting the show to start.
Heads bowed, clasped hands,
A sea of spectators, of eager fans . . .
Quiet anticipation in the dark.

No one moved, no one stirred,
No one took a breath to speak.
The collective excitement was beyond words,
Rising above the stadium like a bird,
The people frozen in their seats.

Down on the field far below
A lone figure stepped into the light.
Dressed in white from head to toe,
His eyes and hair as black as a crow,
He flashed a smile strained and tight.

He held up his hands and addressed the crowd
Without the aid of a microphone.
Even so his voice rang clear and loud,
The air of a man both strong and proud,
His voice deep of timbre and rich of tone.

END OF THE WORLD BENEDICTION

"Welcome to the show, my friends,
I'm so glad to see you here.
Tonight the world as we know it ends,
Scoured away by bitter winds.
But let us not shed a single tear.

The world is a cruel and hurtful place,
So far from the original paradise.
In every heart, in every face,
Is only malice, only hate.
Mankind has become lower than even mice.

So why should we even want to remain
On this floating garbage heap?
Life is disappointment, life is pain.
Man commits atrocities without any shame,
And for lost souls no one weeps.

So we gather here tonight
In an act of ultimate protest.
We'll hear the thunder, see the light
And show the world what is right,
Then we'll find eternal rest."

Those in the stands did not cheer
Or raise their voices in a roar,
But in their silence it was clear
They were united and did not fear,
They were committed to their core.

And so the man on the field
Opened his coat to the blessed.
He did not have a sword to wield,

Nor a mace or a shield,
But explosives strapped to his chest.

Still no movement, still no words,
Just silent conviction.
Not a murmur could be heard,
But some clasped hands in this absurd
End-of-the-world benediction.

When the explosion shattered the night
And washed the stadium from the earth,
No one tried to escape or fight,
Because they knew what they did was right . . .
And through sacrifice had proven their worth.

GOING TO SEE A MAN ABOUT A DOG

ETHAN JAMES WAS only four years old. Too young to know anything of the world outside his limited experience and household.

Therefore, he was too young to know the mobile home in which he lived with his parents was a rundown hovel, one step up from living in a cardboard box. That setting out a dozen or so rusted pots and pans to catch the water leaking through the sagging ceiling was not what everyone did during a rainstorm. That the furry little animals he sometimes saw scurrying under the refrigerator when the kitchen light was turned on were not "pets". That the man he thought of as his daddy was really his stepfather, his real father serving time in prison for armed robbery and aggravated assault.

Most of all, Ethan was too young to know his parents were a couple of lowlife junkies who cared more about their next high than him.

~∖∕~

"Where you going, Daddy?" Ethan asked.

His father paused with one hand on the doorknob, the car keys dangling from the other. Scott "Skeeter"

Boyd was tall and rail thin, his perpetually greasy hair tucked up under a trucker's cap, wearing dirty jeans with rips at the knees and a sleeveless T with the Confederate flag emblazoned across the front.

"Just going to see a man about a dog, little man."

Ethan's eyes widened, and he clasped his hands under his chin. "Are we gonna get a doggie?"

"Uh, maybe. I gotta talk to the man, see how much he wants for it."

"Can I come?" Ethan asked, rushing over to his father and tugging on his pants leg. "Please please please please *please!*"

"Little man, I think you better stay here with your Mama."

"She's sleeping."

Skeeter looked over at his common law wife, Tammy, who was passed out on the sofa, her mouth wide open with a waterfall of drool sliding over her chin. Loud, frog-like snores filled the room. When Tammy took one of her chemically-induced "naps", she was usually out for hours, and nothing short of an atomic bomb going off in the house could wake her. And maybe not even that; it had never exactly been tested.

"Why don't you just stay here and watch some TV? I won't be gone long."

"But I wanna go see the man about the doggie too."

"Fine," Skeeter said, opening the door, "but you have to stay in the truck."

Ethan jumped up and down. "Yay!"

The drive took fifteen minutes, and Ethan kept up a steady stream of questions the entire time. How big was the doggie? What color was it? Did it have a name? Did it know how to fetch, play dead, and roll over?

Skeeter paused before each answer, and it never would have occurred to Ethan's innocent, trusting mind his father was making all this up. As far as he was concerned, his daddy was the greatest man who'd ever lived.

The beat-up Chevy turned down a gravel drive that continued another half mile before dead-ending in a dirt yard with a ramshackle, wood-frame house at its center. A shirtless man covered in tattoos sat on the front steps, smoking a funny little cigarette that winked a red eye in the gathering twilight, but Ethan spared the man only a passing glance. His attention went instantly to an oak tree to the left of the house. Chained to the tree was a Rottweiler, black as the devil's heart. It strained at its chain, barking and snarling at the truck.

"Is that the doggie?" Ethan asked, bouncing in his seat. "Is that the doggie you're here to see the man about?"

Skeeter seemed a bit surprised to see the dog but recovered quickly. "Uh, yeah. You stay here; I'm gonna go in and talk business with him, see if we can make a deal."

"I wanna go pet the doggie."

"No!" Skeeter said sharply, opening his door. "You promised you'd stay in the truck and wait. Don't make me regret bringing you, or you definitely won't be getting no dog."

This quieted Ethan, and he settled in the seat and

put his hands in his lap. "I'm sorry, Daddy. I'll be a good boy."

Skeeter closed the door behind him and walked over to the house.

Ethan watched through the windshield as the two men had a conversation he couldn't hear; then, they both went inside. Ethan turned his gaze back to the Rottweiler, who continued to growl and slobber and bark. The chain was pulled taut, and the dog pawed at the dirt as if trying to uproot the tree to which it was tethered so it could rush forward toward the truck.

Ethan, whose only real experience with dogs came from TV, didn't interpret this behavior as aggressive in any way. He simply thought the doggie wanted to play with him, and he wanted to play with the doggie.

He glanced back at the house. Through the open door, he could see his father sitting on the edge of an old armchair, some kind of tube tied around his arm, and he seemed to be giving himself a shot. Ethan hated shots, couldn't imagine wanting to give one to yourself.

Skeeter was preoccupied with the task at hand, however. Oblivious to all else. Deciding to risk the spanking he'd get for disobeying his father, Ethan opened the door, climbed down out of the truck, and sprinted across the yard toward the dog.

THE SANDBOX

TIMOTHY ELLIS SAT alone in the sandbox while the other kids played nearby. His plastic bucket lay on its side, the tiny shovel stuck in the stand and standing straight up. Timothy trailed his fingers through the soft sand, creating complex and indecipherable symbols. The partially-collapsed tower of an aborted castle crumbled next to him, an outward manifestation of how he felt inside.

Glancing over toward the swings, he saw Bradley Sims and his cronies pointing in his direction and laughing. Even the girls playing jump rope by the bike rack seemed to snicker at him. He should be used to it; this had pretty much been his experience every recess since kindergarten, but the older he got, the more painful the humiliation became.

At seven years old, Timothy had never had a single friend that wasn't imaginary. Almost instantly when he started school two years ago, the other kids had singled him out for ridicule and mockery. As if he gave off some scent that marked him as an outsider. By first grade, he was the butt of everyone's jokes, the one with the "KICK ME" sign perpetually stuck to his back, the target for all the spitball cannons made from straws in the lunchroom.

Why me?

Timothy asked himself that question a lot. What made him such a freak? Sadly, he had a laundry list of possible reasons.

One, he didn't have a daddy. He barely even remembered his father, who had run off with a waitress from the Waffle House when Timothy was only two years old.

Two, he dressed funny. His mother got almost all his clothes secondhand from thrift stores, and none of them fit right. Pants too baggy, shirts too tight, shoes too big with crumpled paper filling out the toes. Last year, Bradley had said in front of the whole class Timothy dressed like a clown, and now everyone at school called him Bozo.

Three, his mother had a reputation around town. She drank a lot, Timothy could attest, and she spent almost every night out at Duvall's, the beer joint downtown. On more than one occasion, Timothy had woken up to find a strange man drinking coffee in the kitchen. Mama always said these men were "good friends", yet he never saw any single one of them more than once.

Four, Timothy was awkward. Tall and gangly, uncoordinated, and totally uninterested in the sports they played in P.E. If someone threw a ball at him, his first instinct was always to move out of the way, certainly not to try and catch it or hit it with a bat. This had earned him the designation of "sissy". Even his mother called him that sometimes.

So, to the other kids at school, Timothy was just a poor sissy with a drunken tramp for a mother and no father, which meant he spent every recess alone in the sandbox making castles . . . at least until Bradley and his crew kicked them over.

Timothy glanced over at the sad mound of the castle he'd started then abandoned, unable to muster the will to work on it anymore. Instead, he continued making lines in the sand with his fingers. A shadow fell over him, and his spine stiffened. He refused to look up, sure it was Bradley or one of the other bigger kids, come to torment him. They'd never actually hit him or anything, just called him names, but Timothy was smart enough to know the "sticks and stones will break my bones, but words will never hurt me" line they liked to feed kids was a load of horse hooey.

"Can I help you with your castle?" a deep, scratchy voice said.

Now Timothy did look up, and an unfamiliar man stood outside the sandbox. He was old, like Grandpa old, with a bald head but bushy white eyebrows and even some hair growing out of his ears like weeds. He stooped slightly, his back rounded, hands buried in the pockets of khaki pants as he smiled at Timothy.

Timothy's own lips pulled down into a frown as he looked past the man, wondering where he'd come from. There was nothing that way but the seesaw and then the fence surrounding the playground, and beyond lay Oakland Avenue. Timothy had never seen the old man before; he wasn't any of the teachers at Oakland Elementary. Maybe a janitor but not one Timothy had ever encountered.

There was something vaguely familiar about him, but maybe he just reminded Timothy of a cartoon character who couldn't see.

"What are you doing here?" Timothy asked. He had

been taught at school never to talk to strangers, but he figured it was okay since he was in the playground with all the other kids nearby. The old man wasn't likely to try and snatch him with so many witnesses.

"Just passing through, saw you sitting here all by your lonesome, thought you might like a little company."

Timothy glanced back over his shoulder at the rest of the kids. For the time being, they had gone back to ignoring him, which was preferable to the taunting. Bradley and his cronies tossed a Frisbee amongst themselves, and the girls who'd jumped rope earlier were now playing hopscotch near the flagpole. The brainy kids sat in a circle on the pavement in front of the main entrance to the school, all with books open before them, probably getting a head start on their homework. No one paid Timothy the slightest attention, and it suddenly hit him with the crushing weight of a cartoon anvil just how very alone he was.

The old man stepped into the sandbox and lowered himself slowly to the ground. He groaned, and his joints popped, but he eventually settled into the sand and reached for the bucket and shovel. He filled the bucket and quickly turned it upside down, flat on the ground, lifting it again with a fluid motion, which left a perfectly shaped mound, wide at the base and tapering closer to the top.

"That's pretty good, mister," Timothy said. He usually couldn't remove the bucket without causing some of the sand to collapse.

The old man shrugged. "Years of practice. Now you try."

Taking the bucket and shovel, Timothy packed it,

turned it upside down, then slowly lifted the bucket, trying not to disturb any of the sand beneath.

"That's your mistake," the old man said. "The slower you go, the more chance you'll cause an avalanche. Better just to lift it straight up, quick as lightning."

"I'm afraid if I do that, I'll just knock the whole thing over."

"Sometimes you will," the old man said with a wink. "But you have to trust yourself. Throw caution to the wind, and take the plunge."

Timothy hesitated, took a deep breath, and then jerked the bucket upward. He gasped when he saw that the mound was intact. "I did it, I did it!"

"Of course you did. You can do anything you put your mind to; just have a little faith."

"Thanks, mister."

"I didn't really do all that much."

"No, I mean . . . thanks for being nice to me."

The old man's eyes filled with sympathy, and he reached out as if to touch Timothy but stayed his hand, letting it fall limply to the ground. "I guess people aren't all that nice to you, huh?"

Timothy dropped his gaze and shook his head. He felt like crying, but he fought hard to hold back the tears. He'd been holding back tears for so long, it was a wonder he hadn't drowned by now.

"I know it's tough," the old man said. "I've been there, but what other people think of you does not define you."

Timothy looked up and tilted his head. "What do you mean?"

"I mean, you're a bright kid, and even more, you're

a decent kid. That is a rare thing at your age; you don't yet know just how rare. You're special."

"You don't even know me."

"But I can tell things about people. Call it a sixth sense. Don't ever let the other kids make you doubt your worth. They're mean to you because they have problems of their own, and sometimes when people are in pain, they lash out at others to make themselves feel better. That has more to do with their character or lack thereof, not yours. All that matters is what you think of yourself."

This gave Timothy pause. What did he think of himself? He wasn't sure. He usually saw himself only through the eyes of others, which didn't add up to a flattering picture.

But what if the old man was right? What if how others viewed him didn't really matter? After all, his mother had proven herself to be wrong more than once . . . maybe she was wrong about him. And Bradley and the other kids, maybe they were wrong too.

"Tell me," the old man said. "What do you like to do?"

Timothy shrugged with one shoulder but then glanced down at the perfect castle tower he'd just made. "Well, I sorta like to build things."

"Like with an erector set?"

"I don't have one of those . . . yet. I'm planning to ask for one for my birthday, but I still have some old Lego blocks from when I was like five that I use to make these whole little towns. I've even used Popsicle sticks and Elmer's glue to put stuff together. Right now, in Art class, we're doing papier-mâché, and Miss Clackston said the house I'm making out of cardboard, newspaper, and that sticky flour-paste is the best in the class."

The old man gave a knowing nod. "I knew I was in the presence of greatness. America's next great architect sits across from me. The next Frank Lloyd Wright."

Timothy laughed, his cheeks flaming with warmth. "I could never be an architect. It takes college and junk."

"Then you go to college and junk."

Timothy shook his head. "Nah, college takes money, and we don't got none of that."

"You don't have *any* of that, and you can always get scholarships, grants, loans if you need to. It's definitely doable."

Another shrug, and the heat in his face intensified. College . . . he'd never considered it a real possibility. His grades weren't terrible, but his mother and the other kids always made him feel stupid, like he wasn't good at anything.

But again . . . what if they were wrong?

"Did you go to college?" Timothy asked, still staring down at the mounds of sand. When no answer came, Timothy looked up to find the old man staring up at the sky with a distant cast to his eyes, as if contemplating the clouds.

"You okay, mister?"

The old man started and then laughed at himself. "Sorry, Tim, but I have to get going."

Disappointment settled over Timothy like a wet blanket. "You sure you can't stay a little longer? We can work on the sandcastle together."

"Afraid not," the old man said with a gentle smile. "I've stayed just about as long as I can."

"Will you be back?"

"Life's a circle; we all come back around eventually."

Timothy didn't know what to make of that, but he kept his silence. Seemed the polite thing to do.

"You're going to be fine, Tim," the old man said with a resolute nod and another wink. "Just believe in yourself even when no one else does."

Timothy looked away again, not wanting the old man to see he was near tears. How ridiculous, to be this broken up about a total stranger, yet this was the first time anyone had ever taken an interest in him. A *real* interest. Even Miss Clackston, who thought his papier-mâché house was the best in the class, sometimes called him Tommy. Odd as it might be, the old man was the closest Timothy had ever had to a friend, and he didn't even know the guy's name.

"Hey, mister, what's your—"

Timothy's words cut off abruptly when he turned to discover the old man gone. Only later, while taking a spelling test, did it occur to him to wonder how the old man had known his name.

―✸―

This memory Timothy clung to decades later as he lay in his deathbed.

Deathbed. A Victorian-sounding word he had rarely heard outside of novels and melodramatic films, but it felt appropriate here. It felt *right*.

For Timothy was dying, of that he had no doubt. Every nerve in his body screamed that his life was winding down, but what really brought reality home were the people gathered around him. His closest friends and family, that was to be expected, but here were faces of relatives he normally saw only once a year, if that. They had all gathered now for a morbid family reunion, to say goodbye to Timothy Ellis before he shuffled off the mortal coil.

But Timothy wasn't sad, at least not overly so. He'd celebrated his ninety-second birthday just last month, had lived a life full of joy, adventure, love, and challenge. He didn't feel entirely ready to go, but he figured he never would. He'd had his share; it would be selfish to expect more.

His thin lips curled in a slight smile as he thought again of the old man in the sandbox. He'd never told anyone of that experience, not sure he would ever be able to fully explain just how transformative it was, how much it had altered the course of his life. Sounded dramatic for such a small moment, but sometimes, the most profound moments of our lives were not grand scenes with sweeping symphonic background music like in the movies but quiet and the importance only recognized in retrospect.

The old man was the first person who ever encouraged Timothy, made him feel he was capable and that his future could be bright. It had motivated him to work harder in school, which helped him earn the scholarships that got him through college and to his degree in architecture. He may not have been the next Frank Lloyd Wright, but he'd done alright for himself. Not to mention a beautiful wife—who had passed seven years prior—kids, grandkids, even a few great-grandkids.

Yes, his had been a full and rewarding life, and he had nothing to complain about. He wanted to tell his family how much they meant to him, how grateful he was they were here, but exhaustion overcame him suddenly, preventing him from speaking. He closed his eyes, thinking, *This is it. On to the next adventure.*

From behind his closed lids, a bright light pierced his eyes. He held up a shielding hand and squinted, wondering why someone had turned on the fluorescents over his bed.

As his eyes adjusted, he found he wasn't staring up at the ceiling but out across a playground. He stood on springy grass, a waist-high chain-link fence at his back. In the distance, he saw a group of boys passing a Frisbee while nearby girls played hopscotch. Another group sat near the school building with books open before them. Apart from all of them, only a few feet from Timothy, sat a lone boy in the sandbox, a crumbling mound of an aborted castle next to him. The boy trailed his fingers in the soft sand, creating complex and indecipherable symbols.

Timothy frowned, momentarily confused and disoriented, but then everything became wholly clear in a brilliant flash of revelation. The frown melted into a smile as he walked toward the boy.

WRONG

WHEN JANET STEPPED into the copier room, the last thing she expected to find was her boss sitting on a box of copy paper crying.

"Oh," Janet said, already backpedaling toward the door. "Carol, I'm sorry, I didn't mean to intrude."

Carol jumped to her feet, flustered, quickly wiping her eyes and nose with a crumpled tissue. "No, it's my fault. I shouldn't be going on like this at work. Very unprofessional of me."

"Don't worry about it," Janet said. She held the spreadsheet she'd been coming to copy against her chest like a shield. "Are you . . . uhm, is everything okay?"

As soon as she asked the question, Janet realized how stupid it sounded. If things were okay, Carol wouldn't be crying in the copier room. The two women stared at one another for half a minute then both broke into nervous laughter.

"Look at me, acting like a silly old biddy," Carol said, taking a compact from her purse and checking her makeup. "I just felt emotion overwhelming me, and this room was closer than the lavatory. Guess I just had to get it out. I'll be okay now."

Janet nodded, looking closely at her boss. At forty-five, Carol was ten years older than Janet, and Janet was surprised to realize she knew almost nothing about the woman other than her age. They weren't what one would call close, but neither did they have an adversarial relationship. It struck Janet as odd she wouldn't have gleaned some information about her boss's personal life over the years.

With her head ducked down like she was expecting a hit, still embarrassed at having been caught in such an emotional moment, Carol started from the room. Janet reached out and stopped the woman with a hand to her arm. "Do you want to talk about it?"

Carol gazed at her with such naked need in her eyes it was almost painful to look at. The older woman took a shuddering breath and said, "My son Jimmy was arrested last night."

"Oh dear, that's horrible. What for?"

Carol kneaded her hands together, and tears welled in her eyes again.

"If you don't want to tell me, it's fine," Janet said.

"No, I won't really be able to keep it a secret much longer anyway. I'm sure it'll be all over the news. Jimmy's accused of raping a girl and then beating her unconscious. She's in a coma, doctors don't know if she's going to make it."

Janet put a hand to her chest—a melodramatic gesture but appropriate. She wasn't sure what to say to such a confession and found herself stammering a response. "That's just . . . I mean, I couldn't imagine. Is he . . . why do they suspect your son?"

"It's a girl he was dating. Her roommate said Jimmy picked her up the night it happened, and that was the last time anyone saw her until she was found in a ditch out on a country road. Jimmy says they got in a fight on the way to the movies, and she demanded he let her out, said she'd walk back to her apartment."

"What a nightmare, but I'm sure the truth will come out, and your son will be cleared of the charges."

Carol snorted a laugh, which turned into a sob. "I think he's guilty."

Janet was sure she misheard. "What?"

"He probably did it. Hell, no probably about it. I'm sure he violated that girl then pummeled her nearly to death. I can only pray he doesn't get away with it."

Janet was flabbergasted, completely stunned by what she'd just heard. "But . . . I mean, he's . . . your son."

Carol smiled, but it was a grotesque sight. "Don't remind me. Tell me, have you ever seen the movie *The Bad Seed*?"

Janet nodded mutely.

"Well, that's Jimmy. Right from the start. If there was trouble to be found, he was into it, and if there was no trouble to be found, he'd create some. I figured it was part of being a boy, you know. Rambunctious, some would call it. I tried instilling him with a sense of values, but he was always getting into fights with the other kids in the neighborhood. At age five, he bloodied the nose of a kid three years older than him and laughed about it, said the boy had it coming for not letting Jimmy play with some toy. He never listened to me or my husband, wouldn't go to bed when we told him to, wouldn't turn the television off when we asked him to, refused to do his homework even if we begged. And no punishment—not grounding or taking away his video games or even spanking—

seemed capable of getting him to fall in line. He just seemed to be born missing something."

"Missing what?" Janet whispered, her voice hoarse.

"The part that told him what was right and what was wrong. He has never seemed to possess it. And as he got older, it got increasingly worse."

"Carol, you don't have to tell me all this if you don't want to."

"No, I want to. It feels good to unburden; I've been keeping it all bottled up for so long. The only person I could ever discuss this stuff with was my husband, Carl, and when he passed three years ago . . . well, I lost my only confidant."

Janet nodded and took a seat on the same box Carol had sat on when she'd first walked in. "When you said it got worse as he got older . . . ?"

"Well, about age eleven, Jimmy started stealing anything that wasn't tied down. Candy and toys from stores, comics and stickers from the kids at school, he even stole some of my makeup and his father's photo albums. It didn't seem to be important what he stole, didn't matter if he had a use for the items or not; he just wanted to take what wasn't his. I think he believed everything belonged to him. He graduated to larger things, like bicycles and video games. When he was fifteen, he broke into a neighbor's house and swiped their TV/VCR. When he was caught and we confronted him, asking why he'd done it, he just shrugged and said, 'Because I wanted it'. Simple as that, he wanted it, and therefore he thought it was perfectly all right to take it. Luckily, the neighbor agreed not to pursue the matter legally since the TV was returned.

"A year later, I caught him with a stray cat. I came home early and surprised him. He was in the backyard and had nailed the cat to an old piece of plywood. It was alive, mind you, yowling something awful, sounding like a baby screaming. He just looked at me and said, 'I wanted to know how long it would take it to die'. I sent him up to his room, and when Carl got home, he put the poor creature out of its misery. Even though by this point Jimmy was bigger than his father, Carl took the belt to him until it raised welts, and Jimmy took every bit of it, never crying out, never displaying any real emotion. I found myself wondering about the Stevenson's dog that had gone missing the previous summer, but I was afraid to ask Jimmy about it. Mostly because I was afraid he'd tell me the truth.

"Things went on from there pretty much the same. Jimmy got into fight after fight, once breaking a kid's arm in a schoolyard brawl. Everyone who witnessed it said the other kid started it, but they also said even after the kid was down, Jimmy kept on kicking him. At eighteen, he stole a car and wrecked it. Got away with just a slap on the wrist and probation. We tried our best to reach him, to turn him back onto the right path, but nothing seemed to get through to Jimmy. I won't lie; my husband and I were both terrified of him, and when he got his own apartment, we were more than happy to see him go.

"And now this. I just know he did what they're saying, and I feel like it's all my fault."

"Carol, no," Janet said. "You did everything you could as a parent."

"Did I really? I don't know, sometimes I wish I'd . . . "

"What? Sometimes you wish what?"

Carol's eyes were raw and red and contained an intensity frightening to behold. "Sometimes I wish I'd drowned him in the tub when he was a baby."

Janet recoiled as if she'd just been slapped. "Oh, Carol."

"I know it makes me sound like a terrible person, but it would have saved so many different people so much pain. I tell you, my boy was born *wrong* somehow, and if I'd only known then what I know now, I could have prevented all this. Just held him under 'til the bubbles stopped."

Janet was too stunned to speak, and the two women sat in silence for several minutes, not quite able to meet each other's eyes. Finally, Carol cleared her throat, pulled out another tissue, wiped her eyes, and blew her nose. "I'm really sorry for laying all this on you, Janet. It really wasn't fair of me."

"No, it's fine," Janet said, feeling dazed.

"Well, enough wallowing. How are you? How's your little one?"

"Oh, he's fine. Quite a handful right now."

"How old is he?"

"Four."

"Well, they're all a handful at that age. You take good care of him."

Janet nodded and said nothing else as Carol left the copier room. When Janet was alone, she wrapped her arms around herself and shivered.

―᠈᠕ᡗ―

Even before Janet got through the front door that night, she could hear her husband Paul yelling. Part of her wanted to get back in the car and drive away, anywhere but here, but instead, she sighed and stepped into the living room.

Their son P.J. stood in front of the TV, holding something behind his back, his face set in a stubborn expression Janet was much too familiar with.

"I said give me the remote," Paul was saying, his voice loud with a lethal edge of exasperation.

P.J. shook his head. "No! I want to watch SpongeBob!"

"I said no TV for you, young man."

"What's going on?" Janet said, not really wanting to know.

"Well, when I picked our son up from daycare this afternoon, I got some bad news. Seems he bit one of the other kids . . . again. This time, he broke the skin, deep enough that it required stitches. They won't have him back. They suggested we send him to a child psychologist, and the kid's parents are threatening to sue us."

"I wanted to play with the Lego blocks, but Deanna was hogging them," P.J. said, stomping one of his feet. "So I bit her on the arm. It's her own fault."

Janet knelt down in front of her son, searching his eyes for . . . she wasn't sure what, but whatever it was, she didn't think she found it. "Honey, you do realize what you did was wrong, don't you? It's never okay to hurt someone else just because they have something you want. Do you understand that?"

"It's her own fault," he said again, throwing the remote he'd been hiding behind his back across the room. It hit the far wall and broke into several pieces.

Janet's shoulders slumped. She was so exhausted. She'd been putting up with this kind of behavior ever since her son had first learned to walk and talk. "P.J., your father is right; no TV for you. You need to be punished."

P.J. lashed out with his little hand and slapped Janet in the face. It stung, but it wasn't the first time.

"Young man!" Paul roared, unbuckling his belt. "You're asking for it."

"Don't," Janet said, taking P.J. into her arms. He struggled, bucking and kicking at her, but she held him tight. "I'll take care of it."

"What are you going to do?"

She looked back at her husband with empty eyes. "Just relax, watch some TV. I'm going to go give P.J. a bath."

EVOLUTION

DRU STRADDLED THE idling Harley, chewing on her bottom lip. "You sure about this?" she asked.

Lowell stood on the broken and buckled sidewalk, hands stuffed in the pockets of his oversized pants. A length of chain threaded through the belt loops. "I'm sure. I appreciate everything you've done for me, but it's time I stand on my own two feet."

Dru sat there a moment longer then nodded, twisted the throttle on the handlebar, and shot down the darkened street without so much as a goodbye.

Watching her go, Lowell felt a sadness settle on his chest like a stone. He wasn't sure exactly how long he'd been traveling with Dru, but he guessed at least half a year. She'd rescued him from a couple of Neanderthals who had been in the process of beating him to death after having already killed Lowell's boyfriend, Rick. She saved his life, provided him with protection while he healed as well as friendship.

Friendship? On second thought, he didn't know if he could classify their relationship thusly. Dru's personality was cold and distant; she spoke little and hardly opened up, yet he sensed beneath the surface, she harbored great sensitivity and compassion. Look at everything she'd done for him, after all.

EVOLUTION

He couldn't rely on her to take care of him forever. The time had come for him to be a man and take care of himself.

He turned and walked toward what had once been the downtown area of the city, back before the Plague had decimated society. He walked through the ruins as a warm breeze sent crumpled, yellow papers scuttling along the cracked pavement, relics of a bygone era. Lowell didn't even remember the world before everything had fallen apart. A world of lights and plumbing and television and internet and laws and boundaries. When he tried to think back on those times, it was like remembering a dream and catching only fragments. The world was now hard and dangerous and the very definition of anarchy.

For the first time in a long while, he was alone in it.

He had gone four blocks, head down with his long, stringy hair hanging in front of his face like a veil, when he heard footsteps behind him. He did not slow his pace or glance over his shoulder, just continued on. He only stopped when he heard more footsteps coming from ahead.

He looked up to see a scrawny man with the beady eyes and the twitchy nose of a rat approaching him. "Looks like we got us a trespasser."

Lowell tensed. "I'm just passing through."

"Well, you's in *our* neighborhood," said a voice at his back. Lowell turned to study the short, doughy man who leaned against a dead lamppost. "Anyone that passes through here's gotta pay a toll."

"What kind of toll?"

"Everything ya got."

"What if I haven't got anything?"

Dough Boy laughed. "Then you in a whole heap of trouble, I'd say."

Rat Face was squinting at him. "Hey, this'un looks familiar. I think we seen him before."

Dough Boy stepped closer, so close in fact Lowell could smell his halitosis. "I think you's right. Hey boy, ain't you the faggot whose butt-buddy we killed a while back?"

Lowell gritted his teeth, assaulted by the painful memories of what these assholes had done to poor Rick. "Yes," he hissed. "That would be me."

Dough Boy clapped his hands and did a little jig, causing his flab to quiver and jiggle. "Hot diggity damn! Thought we'd lost ya when that dyke came swooping in and snatched ya right out of our hands."

"Where is she?" Rat Face asked, his eyes darting around the area.

"She's gone," Lowell said. "It's just me."

Dough Boy grinned so wide it seemed his face might split open. "Goody for us. We's finally get to finish the job we started."

"You don't want to do that."

"Sure we do," Dough Boy said then looked over Lowell's shoulder at his partner in crime. "Take 'im."

Rat Face moved fast, but Lowell was faster. He sidestepped out of the way, ducked the swipe of Rat Face's arm, then came up and rammed his elbow into the back of the skinny man's neck. Rat Face cried out and fell face-first onto the pavement. Lowell grabbed the dangling end of the chain and pulled it through the belt loops in one single motion, letting it swing from his hand like a whip.

EVOLUTION

"Grew some balls, didja?" Dough Boy said, amusement coloring his voice. "Put up a fight all you's want, it'll just make it sweeter when I's take ya down."

From a deep pocket, Dough Boy pulled out a rusty and stained switchblade, but it looked plenty sharp. Lowell didn't wait for Dough Boy to make his move; he lashed out with the chain, which wrapped around the obese little man's wrist. Lowell yanked the chain back, and Dough Boy was dragged along. Lowell held out a fist, Dough Boy's baby face colliding with it. The man dropped like a sack of stones, the switchblade falling from his hand. Lowell kicked it across the street.

Hearing movement behind him, Lowell turned to see Rat Face getting back to his feet. He flicked his wrist, and the chain sailed out, catching Rat Face right across the mouth. The man screamed, blood cascading over his lower lip, and spit out a couple of blackened teeth. He dropped to his knees, clutching at his shattered mouth.

Turning his attention back to Dough Boy, who had managed to push up onto his knees, Lowell wrapped the chain around the man's pudgy neck and cinched it taut. Dough Boy clawed at the chain, twisting his head from side to side, but Lowell kept the pressure firm. The obese little man's face turned an alarming shade of bright red as he spit and sputtered and wheezed.

Rat Face, recovering with commendable speed, launched himself onto Lowell's back, scratching at the man's eyes. Not releasing the chain, Lowell merely leaned forward and bucked the skinny man off him like a dog shaking off a flea. Rat Face flipped over Lowell's shoulder and tumbled into a collection of dented metal garbage bins.

Dough Boy had stopped clawing at the chain, and his hands were flailing around at the debris that littered the sidewalk. Whether by design or by chance, he grabbed hold of a wicked piece of thick, opaque glass, a jagged shard that may have once been part of a liquor bottle. Lowell saw it but not in time to react. Dough Boy stabbed the glass into Lowell's left foot, easily going through the thin material of the moccasin he wore, and penetrated the flesh.

Lowell screamed through gritted teeth, but he only renewed his grip on the chain, pulled it tighter and wrenched violently to the right. Dough Boy's head twisted in that direction as well. Lowell heard a loud *snap*, and the man went limp. Lowell released the chain and let the body keel over.

Glancing over at the garbage bins, Lowell saw Rat Face staring at his companion's body with wide eyes and a slack mouth. A mask of shock and incomprehension. They had spent so much time bullying and tormenting others, they had probably come to think of themselves as invincible.

Lowell took a step forward, and Rat Face scrambled to his feet and started running away. Lowell whipped out with the chain, which wrapped around the scrawny man's ankle, sending him skidding along the sidewalk, knocking his jaw against the pavement, losing a few more teeth in the process.

As Lowell slowly walked forward, he wound the end of the chain around his right hand, creating a makeshift set of brass-knuckles. Rat Face flipped onto his back, pushing up on his elbows. "I'm sorry," he said, his words coming out as a mumble. "I take it back, I take it back!"

Lowell straddled him and dropped down onto his chest, forcing him flat again. "You can't take it back. You can't undo what you did."

Before Rat Face had a chance to say more, Lowell punched him with the chain-wrapped hand, feeling the satisfying crunch of the man's nose breaking beneath the force and weight. He raised his fist and brought it down again. And again. And again.

He didn't stop until Rat Face's countenance had disintegrated into a bloody ruin, barely recognizable as anything human. Some of the blood bubbled up, but when those bubbles popped, no more followed.

Lowell rose to his feet and stayed there, swaying slightly until he heard the sound of an approaching engine that came to a stop behind him. Dru had stayed close by to watch. He hadn't asked her to, but he wasn't surprised.

"Do you feel any better?" she asked.

Lowell looked from one body to the other then up at her. "Yes. I mean, it doesn't bring Rick back, and his loss will always be a blade in my heart, but yes, this made me feel better."

Dru said nothing, just nodded.

"You know," Lowell continued, "when we came up from the coast to scavenge for supplies and spotted these assholes, I considered not pursuing it. I told myself that vengeance was a petty endeavor and that I should take the higher road. That's all bullshit, of course, and it was my fear talking. The fear I have lived with my entire life, but I'm not the same man anymore. This world has no place for fear."

Dru cut the engine and popped the kickstand of her bike, walking over to stand next to Lowell. She placed a hand tentatively on his shoulder but removed it after only a few seconds. "I would have helped, you know."

"I know, but I needed to do this on my own. Of course, it wouldn't have been possible if you hadn't trained me. Thank you."

"Don't mention it. Are you ready to go? We'll have to leave soon if we want to get back to the coast before dark, and I can clean and bind up your foot."

Lowell carefully threaded the chain back through the belt loops then looked at Dru. "When we first met, you told me you weren't really looking for a traveling companion. You took care of me while I healed, but I'm okay now, and because of your generosity, I can take care of myself. If you want to cut me loose, I'll understand."

Dru nodded and said, "So are you ready to go?"

A small smile curling his lips, Lowell followed her back to the bike. Dru threw a leg over the machine, and Lowell climbed on behind her. Wrapping his arms around her waist, he tilted his head back and let his hair blow in the wind as they shot off toward the city limits.

THE BRACELET

BRYANT'S CELL PHONE rang when he was four blocks from home.

He expected it to be Lyle, wanting to know why Bryant was running late, but when he glanced at the screen, he saw it was his friend Fiona calling.

Bryant clicked the button on the Bluetooth plugged in his left ear and said, "Hey Sassy, what's up?"

"Not much, just wanted to check on you guys, see how Lyle is doing."

"Perfection. We went to the clinic again on Wednesday. I don't think the doctors really believed what the tests showed them, but Lyle is one hundred percent cancer free. Total remission. One of the nurses said she'd never heard of anyone with lung cancer as advanced as Lyle's that went into total remission; she called it a miracle."

Fiona chuckled softly. "Well, I'm glad it worked out the way it did."

"You and me both. I really thought I was going to lose him, but now, the future is ours again. We're planning a trip to Italy this summer. We've both always wanted to go."

"Italy? That's going to set you back a pretty penny."

"Who cares? Life is short, and we have to make the most of it."

"Who is this?" Fiona said with a laugh. "Where's that hardened cynic I've known since freshmen year of college?"

"Dead and buried. No more cynicism for me. Now I know the world is full of magic. You've been trying to tell me since the day we met, and you've finally made a believer out of me."

"Just cherish one another, and make the most of this second chance."

"No doubt. Lyle is making a romantic dinner for us tonight, and I stopped off after work and got him a bouquet of chrysanthemums. They're his favorite. We're not going to take a single minute for granted."

"That's good to hear. Has he been wearing the bracelet?"

"Every day. He really loves it, and I can't thank you enough for making it for him."

"It was my pleasure. Now I'll let you get to your romantic evening. Call me tomorrow."

"Will do."

Bryant hung up just as he pulled into the driveway. Whistling to himself, something he hadn't done since he was a kid, he grabbed his briefcase in one hand and the bouquet in the other and walked to the front door.

His lips pulled down in a slight frown when he saw the door was closed. Typically, Lyle always opened the door when it was nearing time for Bryant to get home from work, but not tonight. Maybe it was because Bryant was running late and hadn't called or sent a text. He certainly hoped Lyle wasn't mad, but even if he was, the chrysanthemums would smooth things over.

THE BRACELET

Bryant set the briefcase at his feet as he dug his keys out of his pocket and unlocked the door. He let himself into the living room, expecting to be greeted with the aromas of a home-cooked meal and the sounds of dishes clinking in the kitchen. Instead, there was only the astringent smell of lemon-scented cleanser and silence.

The frown deepened, creating a crease between his eyebrows.

"Babe?" Bryant called out, receiving no answer. Truly becoming concerned, he tossed his briefcase onto the sofa and made his way through the house, calling his husband's name.

He finally found Lyle in the bedroom, lying curled in a semi-fetal position on top of the covers and snoring softly. The glow of a bedside lamp spotlighted his face, and the movement of his eyes beneath the lids suggested he was lost in the midst of a dream. His frown melting into a relieved smile, Bryant sat on the edge of the bed. Still holding the flowers in one hand, he reached out with the other to brush Lyle's hair away from his forehead. The man murmured in his sleep.

Bryant reached out to turn off the lamp, but his hand froze inches from the switch. Something on the bedside table caught his attention. A flash of blue-green like a marble.

Except not a marble. A small, teal bead with a hole running through its center. Next to the bead was a thin, leather cord, knotted at the center and frayed at either end. The bracelet, the one that Fiona had made for Bryant to give to Lyle three weeks ago. Lying on the table, broken.

The way that Bryant's heart felt . . . broken.

"Hey there, sweetie," Lyle said, rolling over and stretching. "What time is it?"

Bryant spared his husband only a cursory glance before turning his eyes back to the broken bracelet. "About half past six."

"I'm so sorry, I meant to make us a nice dinner. I was feeling tired after cleaning house, so I laid down to just rest my eyes, and I guess I conked out."

"That's okay," Bryant said, reaching out and picking up the leather cord. "What happened to the bracelet?"

Lyle threw an arm over his eyes and groaned. "Oh man, I must have knocked it off the nightstand without realizing it, and when I was vacuuming in here, the bracelet got sucked up into the vacuum, and the cord snapped. I feel horrible. Fiona went to all the trouble of making it for me, and I couldn't even take care of it. Maybe we can fix it, twine the ends back together or something."

Bryant didn't respond, just held the cord draped across his palm like a dead worm. He felt cold, as if he'd been buried in an avalanche, while at the same time, he felt heat radiating from his gut as if he'd swallowed a ball of fire.

"I'll get dinner ready," Lyle said, pulling himself to a sitting position on the bed, though his head lolled, and his shoulders slumped. "I just feel so drained; I'm not sure why."

Placing a hand on his husband's chest, Bryant gently pushed Lyle onto his back. "You should rest some more. I'll order us some takeout."

"But this was supposed to be our romantic, at-home date night."

"As long as we're together, it will be."

Lyle reached up and ran his fingers lightly down Bryant's cheek before letting his arm drop back to the coverlet. "You're my hero."

Bryant leaned over and kissed Lyle softly. "Rest now, babe. I'll let you know when the food is here."

"I love you," Lyle said as he rolled back onto his side. He was already snoring again as Bryant stepped out of the room, easing the door closed behind him. Returning to the living room, he pulled out his cell, but instead of calling for pizza or Chinese, he dialed Fiona.

When she answered, Bryant wasted no time on pleasantries. "The bracelet is broken."

"What? How?"

"It doesn't matter how, but it's broken. What does this mean?"

A pause on the other end then Fiona said, her tone mournful, "You know what it means."

Tears threatened to overcome Bryant, but he held them back, burning them away in the heat of undirected anger. "The cancer can't be back, it just can't be! The doctors said he was in total remission; just this past Wednesday, they said it!"

"Bryant, honey, I'm sorry, but the way the spell worked was that the cancer was transferred to the bracelet and housed within it, almost like a prison, but if the bracelet is broken . . . well, then the cancer was released back to its original source. Lyle."

"Then make another one. Make another bracelet."

"I can't."

"Of course you can. It's just a knotted piece of leather with a bead on it, for Christ's sake!"

"Yes, I could make another bracelet, but that's all

it would be . . . a bracelet. I told you this kind of magic is delicate and volatile. It was a one-shot deal. I can't duplicate it, not for the same person."

"Then try another spell."

"There is no other spell for this type of thing. I am so sorry, I truly am, but there's nothing more I can do."

Bryant tossed the phone across the room. It collided with the wall and exploded into several pieces. Falling back onto the sofa, he gave in to the tears, letting them flow like a torrent down his cheeks. He realized he was still clutching the leather cord, and he held it up to dangle before his eyes.

Such a thin strap, yet it had contained so much. It had contained Lyle's entire future.

Bryant wanted to scream out all his anguish and pain, but he resisted the urge for fear of waking Lyle.

Lyle. Maybe they should have told him about the bracelet, about its true purpose, but he never would have believed it. Hell, Bryant hadn't believed it at first, had just figured it was one of Fiona's flaky hippie notions with no basis in reality. He hadn't believed it until it had worked.

And it *had* worked for three glorious weeks. But it was ruined now.

He tried to tell himself that at least they'd had these three weeks. Three weeks they would not have had otherwise.

But it wasn't enough. Sweet Jesus, it wasn't enough.

CLICK BAIT

JOSH SAT AT the desk in his dorm room, staring at the laptop screen as he scrolled through his Facebook feed. The computer *dinged* as a new friend request popped up. Charlotte O'Reilly, a college freshman from Oregon. He didn't know her, and they had no mutual friends, but her profile picture was super hot. He clicked ACCEPT then went to her page to search for more photos. Unfortunately, she only had the one, though she had recently posted a link to a video with the caption, "THIS VIDEO WILL MAKE YOU LOSE YOUR MIND!"

"Yeah, right," he said with a sardonic laugh. He clicked the link, and the video started.

⁓⋇⁓

Two hours later, Josh's roommate Henry returned from class. "Josh, I just got a friend request from this smoking hot babe from Oregon named Charlotte," he said as he came into the room. "You're the only mutual friend I have with her. Who is—?"

Henry stopped abruptly when he looked up from his cell. It took several moments for his brain to process what he saw.

Josh sat in the corner, completely naked, his body

smeared with blood and feces. Gripping a pair of scissors in his hand, he carved strange symbols into the flesh of his thighs. Similar symbols dribbled blood from his chest and arms. He babbled nonstop, and though Henry understood all the words, they didn't make sense strung together the way they were.

"The eagle came down and transformed into the grail, but before I could grab it, it turned into a snake and slithered away. The White Queen and the Red Goddess fought over supremacy by seeing who could swallow the most apples whole, but they both choked and turned blue, so it ended in a tie."

Henry took another step toward his roommate, but when Josh plunged the scissors into his right eye, wearing a smile, Henry screamed and ran out of the room.

A DAY LIKE EVERY OTHER DAY

I woke up in the past this morning.

I got up at the same time,
Put on the same outfit,
Drove the same route to work,
Hitting the same potholes along the way.

At the office,
I did the same paperwork
And exchanged the same pleasantries
With the same coworkers I barely know.
My boss gave me the same dire warnings
And impossible deadlines.
I gave him the same polite assurances
While muttering the same curses
Under my breath.

I left work at the same time,
Stopped by the same fast-food joint
For the same takeout,
And ate in front of the TV
While watching the same
Mindless reality shows.

All the while thinking,
"I've done all this before,
I'm just repeating the same day.
I must have woke up in the past this morning."

But as I lay here in my bed tonight,
Preparing to dream the same worn-out dreams,
I realize that I haven't relived a day from my past.
It is simply that every day
Is like every other day.
Variation is a concept for the young,
Repetition the duty of the old.

And yet . . .

Tomorrow I may hit Snooze
And sleep an extra ten minutes,
Wear something different
And take an alternate route to work,
Avoiding the potholes this time.

At the office,
Maybe I'll start a new project,
Really get to know my coworkers,
Invite them out for a drink sometime.
I'll surprise my boss by having
The reports ready before he asks for them.

I'll possibly take a half-day,
Leaving early so I can try
The new Italian restaurant in town.
Afterwards, perhaps I'll take in a play
At the local community theater.

A DAY LIKE EVERY OTHER DAY

Who knows, I might inquire if they are holding
    auditions
For any future productions.
I had an interest in live theater in my distant youth.

Yes, I think with a smile as I drift off to unfamiliar
    dreams,
Maybe tomorrow morning I'll wake up in the future.

Maybe . . .

THE MAN WHO WATCHED THE OCEAN, or TWELVE STEPS DOWN INTO THE SEA

ISAAC STOOD ON the deck that circled the top of the St. Simon's Lighthouse, staring down at the Atlantic Ocean. The waters were choppy today, looking not blue or even brown but a dispirited gray. Below and just to the right of the lighthouse was a small waterpark, miniature golf course, and then a large, open park with playground equipment, picnic tables, and grills for barbequing. Sometimes when Isaac visited the island, these areas were full of people, and the sounds of laughter and voices raised in good cheer drowned out even the roar of the surf.

But not today. It was early autumn, and a chilly rain fell steadily from a gunmetal sky. The ground below was deserted, and Isaac stood motionless, gripping the iron railing, heedless of his damp clothes and the water dripping from his drenched hair into his eyes. His gaze focused on the waters lapping at the rocks. St. Simon's Island had no beach to speak of; the land merely slopped down into a rocky terrain that met the lips of the ocean in a briny kiss. Off in the distance, perhaps half a mile, was a long dock that led out to a large pier. Despite the rain, some fishermen could be seen casting their lines and dropping nets down into the water.

Between here and there, dotted along the coastline, were small, plank walkways leading to wooden steps that descended into the ocean. Isaac studied the steps closest to the lighthouse, wondering as always what purpose they were meant to serve. He supposed for those who wanted to swim in the ocean, easy access to keep them from scrambling over the rocks.

Behind him, he heard footsteps echoing up the circular staircase, but he did not move until a voice called, "Sir, I'm really going to have to ask you to come down now."

The older gentleman, who manned the lighthouse museum, had been hesitant to allow Isaac to go up at all when he arrived, seeing as access to the lighthouse was usually not permitted during inclement weather. He had finally convinced the man, as there was no wind or lightning accompanying the rain. The fact that Isaac was such a frequent visitor and donated generously to the museum helped to grease the wheels as well.

He had been up here for half an hour, however, and it was time to go. He was ready now.

Following the older gentleman down the one hundred and twenty-nine steps, Isaac found his mind turning back to another beach many years ago, when he had been a mere boy of sixteen. He'd fallen in love with a girl of great beauty and intrigue. He'd known her only briefly but had loved her intensely, though the feeling had not been reciprocated. She carried within her a deep pain and longing he could not touch, and this had led her to walk out into the ocean and never return, leaving Isaac with only mystery and uncertainty and grief.

In the intervening years, she had never strayed far from his mind. He had been with other women, tried to love them, buried himself in work as a means of distraction, but none of it satisfied him. It was shallow where he needed depth, empty where he needed it to be teeming with life, mundane where he needed enigmatic magic.

And so he came to the island almost every weekend to climb the lighthouse and watch the ocean, part of him hoping to see his lost love emerge from the waters and beckon him like a mythical siren.

When they reached the bottom of the stairs and stepped out into the museum, which had once been the lightkeeper's house, the older gentleman, whose name Isaac had never bothered to learn, asked, "Would you like a towel? You're sopping wet."

Isaac smiled and shook his head. "I'll just get wet again when I go outside."

"It really isn't the weather for lighthouse gazing, I'm afraid. Feel free to stop by tomorrow; it's supposed to be clear and sunny."

"I won't be around," Isaac said then took the man's hand, squeezing it firmly. "I think I've made my last visit to your lovely lighthouse."

"Moving?"

"Yes, it's time."

"Well, that explains why you were so determined to go up despite the weather. If you ever get back around this way, be sure to visit us again."

"I will."

Isaac left the museum, walking into the downpour. He no longer felt the cold; he was sufficiently numb already. Instead of turning left toward the lot where he'd parked his car, he headed to the right, toward the ocean.

At the first walkway, he stopped at the top of the steps. A dozen total, leading into the churning waters. The three at the bottom had rubber attached to them to prevent people from slipping when those steps got wet. Isaac started down, one hand lightly gripping the wooden railing. The sound of the waves beating against the rocks rang like voices, a multitude of excited whispers. He listened for a familiar voice, but it was impossible to single out just one in the din.

As he neared the bottom, he saw a shadow moving through the water, swimming past the steps. It could have been a large fish or his imagination.

Or something else.

He did not pause or hesitate as he reached the rubberized steps but continued forward, plunging his feet into the water. There were more steps below the surface, and he soon found himself submerged to his waist. He'd thought himself numbed to the cold, but it was as if his lower body had become encased in ice. He did not allow this to stop him.

He spotted the shadow gliding through the water again, now moving away from the coastline and out toward open sea. He couldn't be sure, but he thought he detected the curvaceous shape of a woman. She wanted him to follow her, and he was ready. It was time.

"I'm coming, my love," he said and let himself sink into the ocean.

THE DESK

NICK HENSON NOTICED the desk as soon as he stepped into the back bedroom. The space had apparently been used as some sort of office—a few rickety bookcases against the walls, a dented file cabinet, and shoved in the far corner stood the massive, oak, roll-top desk.

He went to the desk and stroked the top of it. His fingers came away streaked with dust, which he absently wiped on his pants. Like the house itself, the desk was on the shabby side but still beautiful underneath the neglect.

From the doorway, Ellen Johnston said, "Uncle Brady had that old thing for as long as I can remember."

Nick tore his gaze from the desk and back to the skittish woman in the simple blouse and floor-length skirt. With her salt-and-pepper hair pulled up in a bun on the top of her head, she seemed a relic from a more gentile time.

"I've always wanted a roll-top desk," he said.

"Well, I'm planning to donate most of this furniture to the Salvation Army. If you did decide to take the house, I'd happily leave any items you wanted. At no additional cost, of course."

Nodding, he walked around the room, taking in the faded pastel wallpaper. That would definitely have to go. He noted the lighter squares here and there; of course, Ellen would have taken any photographs or other personal items, yet she had left an antique secretary's desk. Perhaps she didn't know what a treasure she had on her hands. Nick could tell her . . . or he could keep his mouth shut and take the desk for himself. She already said if he didn't want it, she was going to donate it to the Salvation Army.

You're talking as if you've already decided to buy the house.

If he were honest with himself, he had. He liked the Craftsman architecture, the built-in bookcase in the living room next to the brick fireplace, the canted bay windows with cushy window seats—even though the cushions themselves needed to be replaced. It was in a quiet neighborhood and within his price range. Actually cheaper due to it being a fixer-upper. And having the desk thrown into the bargain certainly didn't hurt.

Ellen led Nick across the hall, through the kitchen, and out onto the enclosed back porch. From there, she took him into the backyard bordered by overgrown shrubbery. A stone birdbath was planted in the center, chipped and dry. At the very back of the property, half-hidden in the brush, was an old brick grill that had seen better days. Turning back to the house, he surveyed the flaking paint and the missing shingles. The place needed some work, but it wasn't anything he couldn't handle.

"If you don't mind me asking," Nick said, "when did your uncle pass away?"

Ellen wrung her hands, her head tucked in as if she expected a punch. "It's been almost a year now. I wasn't surprised he left the house to me—I was his only family—but I just don't have a use for this place. Thought about renting it out, but I simply can't afford the upkeep, so I put it on the market. The money would come in handy, that's for sure. Not that I'm playing the sympathy card to pressure you into buying the house or nothing."

Nick laughed. "I never thought that. It really is a great house."

"Well, Mr. Henson, how long have you been looking for a place?"

"I haven't. I mean, I've been toying with the idea. I've kind of outgrown my apartment, and I figure thirty-two is old enough to start being an adult. But I hadn't actually contacted a real estate agent or anything, and then yesterday, I had to take a detour on my way to the drugstore because of road construction and came through this neighborhood. I saw the 'For Sale by Owner' sign out front of the house, called the number, and here we are."

"What do you do for a living?"

"I'm a writer."

"Oh, anything I might have read?"

"My first novel came out earlier this year. *Raindrops in the Wind.*"

"Yes, I think I remember hearing about that one," Ellen said, but the blank look in her eyes told a different story. Nick wasn't offended. While *Raindrops* became a surprise bestseller and earned him a pretty hefty advance from Doubleday for his second book, it was still a first novel with no movie deal, so the general public likely wouldn't be aware of him or his work.

"I appreciate you taking the time out of your day to show me the house," he said as they made their way around to the front.

"My pleasure. Since I put the sign up four months ago, there's been surprisingly little interest."

Nick stopped at his car and then smiled at the woman. "Well, I think your luck is about to change."

—━━

Nick sat at the desk in a metal folding chair, his laptop open before him, a blank white page except for a few lines of text and a cursor that mocked him with each blink. He stared around the room, looking for something to distract him from his own unproductiveness, but he'd finished unpacking two days ago and had cleaned the place in such an obsessive-compulsive manner that he'd be hard-pressed to find a speck of dust anywhere. He'd fixed the broken drawer in the kitchen, replaced the shower rod, put up new wallpaper in almost every room, and even planted some azalea bushes along the front of the house. Anything to avoid that damn blinking cursor.

His cell phone buzzed next to the laptop, skittering across the desk's surface. He knew even before looking at the display what name he would see. Bruce Powers, his editor at Doubleday. He'd want a progress report on the new book.

With a flick of his finger, he sent the call to voicemail. He wasn't in the mood to admit to Bruce that he wasn't going to make the deadline, which had already been extended for him once.

"What's wrong with me?" he said, pushing away from the desk. *Raindrops in the Wind* had come relatively easy, taking him only two months to complete the first draft. He'd been working on the new book, tentatively titled *And All that Followed*, for almost six months and was maybe halfway through.

Of course, the difference was *Raindrops* had been written with no deadline, no one waiting on it, and nothing to live up to. He'd written that book primarily for himself, dreaming of it being published but not really expecting it to be.

It had been published, and successful to boot, which was wonderful but also brought with it a great deal of pressure and expectation that seemed to freeze him up. Instead of dealing with that, he looked for distractions to keep him away from the laptop.

The phone chimed, alerting him to the new voicemail. He considered listening to it but instead slid open the small drawer along the front of the desk, dropped the phone inside, then closed it. He found himself staring at the large drawer that made up the bottom half of the base on the right side of the desk. The only locked drawer and for which Ellen hadn't had a key.

He'd considered using the claw end of a hammer to pry it open but didn't want to damage the desk, and he kept meaning to call a locksmith to see if they could make a key for it, but he hadn't gotten around to it yet. He thought about the few moldering boxes and the oversized trunk in the attic and wondered if there might be a key in any of those.

Of course, what he really needed to do was get back to work on the novel . . . so he stood up and headed for the stairs to the attic.

THE DESK

—⁖—

The attic had a low ceiling, a single bulb hanging from the center providing a spotlight of illumination and leaving all the corners in shadow. Nick had placed a few items up here—an exercise bike he'd purchased and used maybe twice, some old textbooks he'd kept from his college years, as well as Christmas and Halloween decorations. Shoved into the back corner were two ripped cardboard boxes and a large travel trunk with a busted lock. These were not his.

They must have belonged to Brady Johnston, and Ellen somehow missed them when she cleared out the house prior to the closing. Nick had been meaning to call her—he had her card somewhere around here— but had yet to get around to that too. After dragging the items into the light, he knelt down in front of the boxes, feeling like a criminal about to rummage through someone else's belongings, but he reminded himself that he'd bought the house and everything in it, so technically, whatever he found inside the boxes and the trunk belonged to him now. Of course, if he found anything personal or valuable, he'd be sure to call Ellen and let her know.

The first box contained musty clothing, mostly seersucker pants and button-up shirts; a strong stench of mildew wafted out. The second box housed a collection of chipped and broken figurines, knickknacks, and various bric-a-brac. That left only the trunk.

Pushing open the lid and peering inside, Nick's breath caught in his throat. As a writer, he'd always avoided using that phrase because he didn't believe it ever really happened, but now, he experienced it firsthand and realized sometimes clichés were also truth.

His breath returned, but he remained crouched over the trunk, like Pandora mesmerized by the evils she'd unleashed. Though no evil resided in this box, or if so, it had long since been released. The only thing inside was a black typewriter.

The old manual kind, large and clunky. A Remington according to the nameplate at the top. He saw the rows of typebars, gleaming like a metal smile, bracketed on either end by the ribbon spools. Nick reached inside, grasped the sides, and hauled it out. The thing was even heavier than he'd been expecting, and he groaned as he hefted the thing over the rim of the trunk and sat it with a *thump* on the floorboards next to him. A thin layer of dust covered the machine, but otherwise, it was in excellent shape. If he had to guess, he'd say the typewriter dated back to the 30s. As a writer, while Nick would never give up the convenience of his laptop, he harbored a great affection for the writing instruments of the past, which explained the quill-and-ink set in the ornate wooden box on the mantel in the living room—it had cost him almost a hundred bucks. He never used them; he just liked to look at them. He'd always wanted a manual typewriter as well, but those puppies went for several hundred dollars. The good ones anyway. It seemed silly to invest so much cash in something obsolete, but now, he had one just drop into his lap.

Don't forget, you said if you found anything valuable, you'd contact Ellen Johnston and return it to her.

Not ready to face the voice of his conscience, he glanced back in the trunk to see if any other treasures waited inside. He found a few extra spools of ribbon, several bottles of Liquid Paper—

—and a set of keys on an O-shaped ring.

"Jackpot," he said, snatching them up. He considered hauling the typewriter downstairs, but he wasn't quite in the mood for the manual labor it would require, so instead, he doused the light and rushed back down the narrow steps, leaving the door to the attic open.

Back in his office, he pulled the chair up in front of the drawer and tried the keys in the lock. The third one fit and turned smoothly. He scooted back and pulled open the drawer. It was deep inside and filled with stacks of paper all the way to the top. He figured they were probably insurance papers, tax records, and other financial documents.

However, upon closer inspection, he saw the paper on top looked like a title page. Big block text, no doubt typed out on the Remington in the attic. "MIRACLES ARE A DIME A DOZEN" centered about halfway down the page, and just underneath that, "By Brady Eugene Johnston".

Intrigued, Nick grabbed up a sheaf of the slightly yellowed pages and flipped through them. Yes, definitely a story of twenty typed pages. He read the first couple of pages, the tale of a young girl named Bethany who runs away from home to search for God. The story contained a fantastical element as she ran into various mythological creatures ranging from satyrs and centaurs to Santa Claus and the Easter Bunny on her quest.

He turned to the drawer and dug through the pages. They were all stories, most of them short fiction but a handful of actual novels as well. Funny how Ellen hadn't mentioned that her uncle had been a writer.

Moving the chair aside, Nick sat on the floor and separated the pages, making stacks for individual stories. He became so engrossed in what he was doing, he didn't even realize more than an hour had passed as the stacks grew around him. He'd definitely found something to distract him from his own writing.

Once he finished separating the stories—one hundred and sixty-five short pieces, five novels, and thirty-two poems which he put together in a single stack—he returned to "Miracles are a Dime a Dozen". He wanted to know how the story ended.

Nick sat up in bed, his back pressed against the headboard, papers strewn all over the coverlet. In the last two days, he'd read half of Brady Johnston's short stories and just finished one of the novels. *The Early Harvest*, a coming of age tale about a young boy growing up in the depression era south. The story was rich and emotionally complex, full of characters that were neither saint nor villain but complicated combinations of both. Though full of melancholy and at times outright heartbreak, the piece also contained some surprising bright notes of humor, striking the perfect tonal balance.

For several minutes, Nick didn't move, just stared down at the words THE END typed at the bottom of the last page. "Damn," he finally said. He felt a mixture of exhilaration and envy, knowing he'd never write anything half as good as the worst of what Johnston had produced.

And which he'd apparently never had published.

Nick had Googled the name "Brady Eugene Johnston" and come up with nothing but the man's obituary. Thinking Johnston may have decided to use a pseudonym, Nick then tried searching several titles, and while he got hits on a few, none of the descriptions matched the stories themselves. As far as Nick could tell, none of these stories ever saw print.

On the nightstand, his cell phone buzzed, indicating he had a new voicemail waiting. No doubt just another in a string of increasingly irritated messages from Bruce. Doubleday was growing impatient, and Nick feared they may invoke the "breach of contract" clause in their agreement, pulling the plug on *And All that Followed* and demanding the advance back, which would be disastrous as he'd already spent half of it.

"What am I doing?" he muttered to himself. "I need to get off my ass and get this book finished."

Of course, he'd been telling himself the same thing for months. On a good day, he mustered a page or two, and on a great day, he didn't go back and delete them. He'd written *Raindrops in the Wind* with such confidence; after the success of that novel, one would think his confidence would only have grown.

The reverse had happened. He felt unsure of himself and his talent. Glancing back at Brady Johnston's novel, the thought repeated: *I'll never write anything half as good.*

Sadness settled over him as he thought about the man in whose home he now lived. He had penned such wonderful stories; why had none of them ever been published? Had he suffered from his own bouts of insecurity and never found the nerve to submit them, or had he just run into shortsighted editors who couldn't recognize his genius? Either way, he'd died never receiving the recognition he should have. Nick figured it was entirely possible that no one even knew these stories existed.

An idea shot through Nick like a lightning bolt, a sudden inspiration that sent him jumping out of bed. He snatched up his cell and hurried to the kitchen. Every house had the obligatory "junk drawer", a sort of catch-all where everything that didn't have a proper place of its own ended up, and Nick's was no exception. He pawed through batteries, candles, spools of thread, a plastic box full of different sized screws, scissors, shoe polish, finally locating the item he needed.

A small card with Ellen Johnston's phone number on it.

He dialed quickly, hoping it wasn't too late to be calling. Nine-fifteen in the evening seemed early to him, but he tended to be a night owl by nature. The line rang three times, and he prepared to leave a message when her timid voice answered, "Hello?"

"Hi, Ellen. This is Nick Henson."

"Oh, hello there. Is everything okay? Something wrong with the house?"

Nick could tell by her tone it had been too late to call, that in her household calls coming after eight usually only meant bad news.

"No, nothing's wrong," he assured her. "I was just up in the attic and found some things that I think must have belonged to your uncle."

"I see. What sorts of things?"

"Mostly clothes and figurines but also an old typewriter. A Remington."

"Oh yes," she said, her voice coloring with delight. "I remember that thing. He used to keep it on his desk—well, *your* desk now—and the typewriter was so big he couldn't roll the top closed."

"Do you have any idea what he used the typewriter for?"

"Correspondence mostly, I'd imagine. In fact, I think I still have some old letters he wrote my mother on it."

Nick leaned against the counter, pressing the phone tightly against his head. "I was just wondering, was your uncle a writer?"

"Writer? You mean as in fiction, like you do?"

"Yeah. Are you aware of him having any ambitions in that regard?"

She laughed, a surprisingly girlish giggle. "Uncle Brady? No, not that I'm aware of. I mean, he was a big reader—I know that much—but I don't think he tried his hand at writing himself. If he had, I'm sure he would have mentioned it to my mother or me."

Nick thought about all the stories he'd read over the past two days by Brady Johnston, stories apparently written in total secrecy and not even mentioned to his family. Quite the twist of fate that had brought two writers to live in this house. One who'd spent his life writing bestseller quality material but then hid it away in a drawer only to die unrecognized, the other who'd lucked into early success but then suffered crippling writer's block that could potentially ruin the career he'd started. Cruel twist of fate indeed.

He became aware that he'd let the phone drift away from his ear, but he could hear Ellen's tinny voice calling his name.

"I'm sorry," he said. "My mind wandered for a moment."

"Well, it's getting late. I was just about to call it a night when the phone rang. You can trash what's up in the attic or donate it to Goodwill, whatever you want. Feel free to keep the typewriter; I don't have much use for it."

Nick thought again of Brady Johnston's stories, the potential in those pages, and smiled.

～ﾍI✦ﾍ～

Taking a seat at the desk, Nick booted up the laptop and opened Google Chrome. From his Bookmarks, he selected the page for the *New York Times* bestseller's list. Top 20 came up, and he scanned the list quickly.

There it was at number 15. *The Early Harvest.*

The novel had been released from Doubleday just over a month ago. Thanks to some aggressive advanced press and several high-profile rave reviews, *The Early Harvest* debuted at number 7 on the bestseller's list, lingering in the top 10 for three weeks, and remaining in the top 20 for the last two. Not too shabby. A burst of pride shot through Nick, making him feel warm all over.

His phone buzzed in his pocket, and he pulled it out, checking the Caller ID before answering. "Well hello there."

"Did you see it? Did you see it?"

"Yup, number 15."

"I can't believe it's still on the list and after a

month. Is that normal? I mean, for someone who didn't write a series about a child wizard?"

"It's impressive, especially for a first novel," Nick said.

Ellen laughed, sounding more like a schoolgirl than the schoolmarm he'd thought she looked like when he first met her. "I guess it must be good. Doubleday has offered a contract for two more of Uncle Brady's novels as well as a collection of his short stories."

"That's great, Ellen. I'm so happy for you."

"I have you to thank for all of this."

"Hey, no need to thank me. It's your uncle's talent that is making all this happen."

"Yes, but you're the one who found the manuscripts I didn't even know existed. Then you set me up with your agent and even a contact at Doubleday. I can't thank you enough."

"Please, I didn't do all that much. Introducing you to those people wouldn't have mattered a bit if your uncle hadn't had the goods to get them interested."

Didn't hurt that Brady Johnston was dead, Nick thought but didn't say. It might be a sad commentary on the publishing industry, but he knew the idea of releasing something posthumously could garner more attention than something by a first-time author who was still breathing. Publishers loved a gimmick because they were easy to sell, but Nick figured selling a gimmick wasn't such a bad thing when there was talent to back it up.

Talent like Brady Johnston had possessed.

"Please forgive me," Ellen said suddenly. "I'm just prattling away, I forgot to mention that I finished your book yesterday."

Nick's smile faltered a little. "What did you think?"

"It was quite good," she said, but her voice lost some of its vibrancy.

"Ellen, you don't have to lie to spare my feelings."

"I'm not lying; I really did like it except . . . well . . . the ending seemed a bit rushed. Left me feeling a bit like the buildup hadn't amounted to much."

Anticlimactic is the word you're looking for, and some of the reviewers agreed with you.

Not that it should be all that surprising that the ending felt rushed. Nick had, after all, blazed through the last third of the novel in only two weeks, determined to make good on his commitment to Doubleday.

And All that Followed had been released two months ago to lukewarm reviews and so-so sales. Not a total disaster but disappointing compared to the sales of *Raindrops in the Wind*. It peaked at number 20 and quickly dropped off the bestseller's list. Possibly the amount of time it had taken to get the book out, losing the momentum of his debut's novel's buzz, had done irreparable damage, but more than one reviewer had utilized the phrase "sophomore slump". Doubleday had chosen not to exercise the option in their contract with Nick, effectively ending their working relationship.

Nick was upset though not as much as he'd thought he would be. Part of him was relieved to have that pressure taken off his shoulders. He thought he now understood why Brady Johnston had worked in secret, telling no one about his writing.

Freedom.

Nick's current project was a novella about siblings

dealing with the loss of their parents called *Mourning Time*. He knew the prevailing wisdom was that novellas didn't sell. He focused only on the story, the joy of getting swept away in a fictional world. He'd lost that with *And All that Followed*; he was glad to discover it wasn't lost permanently. Once the novella was completed, he'd turn it over to his agent to try to find a home for it. Maybe a small press. He'd learned something valuable from Brady Johnston, something he'd once known but lost sight of for a while.

"I hope I didn't offend you," Ellen said through the phone, bringing Nick back to the moment.

"Not at all. I always prefer an honest critique over a polite one."

"Just know I'll be buying everything you put out."

"Thanks, and let me know when Brady's next book is released."

"Absolutely."

After hanging up, Nick sat staring at the bestseller's list for several moments. That warm feeling continued to spread through his body. His smile returning full-force, he pulled up the manuscript for *Mourning Time* and got back to work.

WHEN GAS WAS 52 CENTS PER GALLON

THE CAR STARTED sputtering as they rounded a curve in the rutted, two-lane highway.

"What the *fuck*?" Joe growled from behind the wheel of the Honda.

In the passenger's seat, Brandon gripped the door handle, his whole body tensing. "I think maybe we should pull over."

"Pull over? We're in the middle of Butt-fuck Egypt."

"Well, I don't think we have much of a choice."

As if Brandon's words had been prophetic, the engine cut out with a rattle, and all the dashboard lights glowed blood red. "*Fuck!*" Joe shouted, slapping his hands on the steering wheel.

Brandon leaned forward and pointed out the windshield. "There's some kind of parking lot up ahead. I think we can make it."

Joe managed to coast the car into the small lot of what the headlights revealed to be a long-abandoned gas station. The Honda's forward momentum finally gave up the ghost in front of the old pumps, which looked like robots from some 50s sci-fi movie. A few feet back from the pumps stood a ramshackle building with a large, plate-glass window sporting a spider web of cracks at its center. The door was boarded over and the roof partially caved in.

"Christ," Brandon said, "wonder how long since this place was in business."

"Pretty long time judging by that."

Brandon followed Joe's gaze to a rusty sign swinging above the pumps that announced you could fill up with unleaded for only fifty-two cents per gallon.

Brandon whistled softly. "Man, can you imagine paying so little for gas?"

But Joe was no longer interested in the price of gas. He turned the key rather violently in the ignition, repeatedly. The engine made a grinding noise like it wanted to turn over but just didn't have the strength.

Joe continued his assault on the steering wheel. "Goddamn it all to motherfucking hell!"

Brandon sat quietly, still gripping the door handle. In the past six months that he and Joe had been sharing a dorm room, he'd witnessed his roommate's temper quite a few times and had learned it was best to just make himself as invisible as possible until it passed.

This tantrum lasted about five minutes, leaving Joe panting as he leaned his head back against the seat and let his hands fall limply into his lap.

"So," Brandon said when he judged it okay to speak, "should we look under the hood or something?"

"I don't know what good it would do. I know fuck-all about cars, and I doubt you know much more."

"I know a little."

"Really? Like what?"

"Well, I know they have four wheels."

Joe just stared at him before a laugh sputtered from his lips. "You're a nut, you know that?"

"So I've been told," Brandon said with a laugh of his own. Then, "What do you want to do now?"

Joe cut the headlights and looked over at him, and in the gloomy interior of the car, his face was a mask of shadow. Silence stretched between them, and Brandon was overcome with the conviction that his roommate was about to grab him and plant a kiss on his mouth.

Instead, Joe pulled out his cell and said, "I'm gonna call roadside assistance; what do you think?"

As Joe dialed the number and gave whoever answered directions to send a tow truck, Brandon let out a shaky breath and chastised himself for his own stupidity. *When are you going to stop this idiotic fairytale fantasizing? Joe is as straight as they come, and chances are you wouldn't even be friends if fate hadn't made you college roommates. Yeah, he took you to a concert tonight, but it's not like you're on an actual date or anything. Stop mooning over him like some lovesick girl!*

"All right," Joe said, stuffing the phone back in his pocket. "They said someone will be out in twenty minutes to an hour."

Brandon nodded. "At least it's not too cold out tonight."

"What, you sad you won't have to cuddle up with me for warmth?" Joe said with a laugh, reaching out and lightly punching Brandon in the forearm.

Joe made a lot of jokes like that, so often that Brandon sometimes wondered if there was more behind the comments. Maybe a little bit of truth hiding behind humor.

That's just more of your wishful thinking. You're never going to learn, are you?

"Dude, why are you squirming in your seat like that?" Joe asked.

Brandon hadn't even been aware he was squirming until his roommate pointed it out. "Nothing, I just need to pee."

"Then go pee."

Brandon stared out at the rundown building again. "I guess there would be a bathroom in there, but I don't know how I'd get in."

With another laugh, Joe said, "Just go in the parking lot, doofus, but make sure you aim the spray *away* from the car."

"I can't use the bathroom in the middle of a parking lot. What if someone drives by?"

"We haven't seen another car on this road for almost an hour. That's the whole reason I decided to take the back way on the return trip to campus, to avoid all the crazy traffic on the interstate. Just get out and drain it."

"I don't know."

"Fine, then go around behind the building and take a piss in private."

"That's okay; I can hold it."

"That so?"

Five minutes ago it might have been so, but now that the pressure in Brandon's bladder had become a topic of conversation, it was all he could think about. What had been a mild discomfort moments before was suddenly a painful stabbing in his groin.

"Oh hell," he said, fumbling the door open.

"Don't get lost out there," Joe called after him. "And watch out for bears. By that I mean fat, hairy queers that wanna make you their bitch!"

Ignoring this jibe, Brandon hurried across the cracked and buckled pavement, sliding around the side of the building to the back. Here, the land slopped away steeply to a wooded area. Brandon scanned the darkness, making sure he was alone, and then reached down to unzip his pants . . .

. . . but froze with his hands on his fly. He just couldn't bring himself to go to the bathroom outside, even if he was fairly certain there was no one around. Glancing back toward the building, he saw a back door, and while it may have once been boarded over like the one around front, the boards had been pried off and tossed into a sloppy pile.

Probably teenagers who need a place to drink and smoke and fool around. Or maybe some homeless person.

Brandon had walked toward the door but paused at this last thought. If a homeless person had sought shelter inside the old gas station, it was possible they were still inside. Sometimes, the homeless were just people down on their luck, but sometimes, they were people with severe mental problems that belonged in institutions.

Another stab of pain and the fear of wetting himself made the decision for him. He pulled the door open on creaky hinges and entered the dark building. He fumbled for his cell phone and turned on the flashlight app, a swath of white cutting through the black.

He appeared to be in some sort of storage room,

dusty metal shelves that held a few moldering cardboard boxes and cobwebs. He heard scuttling sounds around his feet but didn't dare shine the light at the floor. He'd rather not know; sometimes, ignorance truly was bliss.

He walked through another doorway into what had once been the store. A few empty shelving units were pushed against the walls, and off to the right was a counter with an ancient-looking cash register on top of it, draped in spider webs as if covered in delicate lace. The floor was carpeted with candy bar wrappers, potato chip bags, crushed soda and beer cans, cigarette butts with roaches the size of baby hands scurrying amongst all the refuse. The walls were spray-painted with obscenities, graffiti tags, and crude depictions of genitalia. Obvious proof that the old gas station was populated at times though it seemed deserted right now.

In the far left corner, Brandon spotted the stick figures indicating restrooms. The one wearing a dress was closer, and though it was silly considering where he was, he passed it by and went into the men's room.

It was a cramped area, like a coffin laid on its end. A rust-stained sink with a cabinet underneath and a lone toilet were all it contained. The toilet no longer held any water, but Brandon tucked his phone under his arm and quickly unzipped and relieved his aching bladder into the empty bowl, sighing as the relief rushed over him.

He urinated for what felt like an hour before he tucked himself back in his pants and zipped up. He jerked and nearly dropped his phone into the toilet when he heard a clattering from out in the store. He felt frozen in place, as if he'd caught a glimpse of Medusa and been turned to stone, but his heart trip-hammered in his chest, and his breath rasped in and out of his lungs.

"Joe?" he said, his voice small and timid. "Is that you?"

Silence answered, but it didn't mean Joe wasn't out there. It wouldn't be the first time his roommate had pulled a prank on him. On Halloween, Joe had hidden under Brandon's bed and jumped out and scared the shit out him. Even more embarrassing was the fact that Brandon had just been about to slip his pants off and play with himself a little, though hopefully Joe didn't realize that had been the intended use for the hand lotion next to the bed.

Brandon crept out of the bathroom, holding up the phone to scan the store. Almost instantly, he spotted the cause of the noise. The cash register had fallen from the counter and was now lying on its side on the floor. No way had an errant breeze knocked the heavy thing over. Someone had to be in this building with him. Probably Joe pulling another prank, but Brandon couldn't be sure. He just wanted to get the hell out of here and back to the car.

Staying close to the back wall, Brandon made his way toward the exit, moving quickly. He was just about to go through the doorway into the storage area when someone grabbed him from behind and dragged him back into the store. The phone fell from his hands, clattering to the floor and extinguishing the light, shrouding the interior in total darkness. A rough hand clamped over his mouth, and Brandon flailed out with his arms and legs to break free.

His assailant's other hand came around and groped at Brandon's crotch, finally sliding down the waistband of his pants and underwear to fondle his dick and balls. Brandon instantly stopped struggling, and his knees went as weak as the cliché about going weak in the knees.

At nineteen, Brandon was still a virgin, and this was the first time anyone had touched his junk other than himself, and the feel of those fingers teasing and squeezing and twisting and pulling was electric. He stiffened under the manhandling, and the hot breath he felt on the back of his neck further enflamed his passions.

This is it; it's finally happening! I'm getting what I've dreamed about for six months! Why Joe chose to make his move in a dirty old gas station crawling with bugs and rats I don't know, but I'm not going to complain.

The hand pulled out of his pants, and Brandon actually let out a soft whimper of disappointment. The other hand came away from his mouth, and he was shoved to his knees. He went with no resistance, a mixture of fear and excitement sending a tingling throughout his entire body.

He couldn't see Joe beyond just a vague shape, a deeper shadow in the darkness, but he heard the grating sound of a zipper being unzipped and the whisper of his pants being dropped. When Brandon felt the hard cock pressed against his lips, he opened his mouth obediently and let Joe slide himself inside. The flesh radiated a surprisingly intense heat, and the musky smell was intoxicating. Brandon sealed his lips tight around his roommate's cock as Joe plunged it down his throat.

Joe's cock was big, long, and thick, and Brandon immediately started gagging and tried to back away, but Joe grabbed him by the back of the head and forced him to stay in place as he continued skull-fucking him. Brandon choked and tried to keep from throwing up, tears streaming from his eyes . . . but his erection was as fierce as ever. He undid his pants and started stroking himself.

Joe suddenly pulled back, sliding his dick out. Brandon, a line of drool dribbling down his chin, made a mewling sound and leaned forward to get another taste. A hand twined in his hair and shoved his face into Joe's balls. Brandon licked and sucked at them, enjoying the flavor of his roommate's sweat. Little hairs got caught between his teeth, but he didn't care. Joe crushed his face so tightly against his crotch Brandon could barely breathe, but he didn't mind that either. If he had to die, there were much worse ways to go out.

His roommate grabbed him by the hair again, jerked him up and dragged him over to the counter, bending him over it before yanking his pants and underwear down to his ankles. For the first time, the fear Brandon felt started to eclipse his excitement.

"Joe, be gentle okay," he said in a breathless voice. "You got any lube or—"

Brandon's words were cut off when a hand clamped over his mouth again, then he felt two fingers roughly entering his anus, stretching and probing and ripping at his hole. He screamed into Joe's palm, the sound muffled and weak, and tried to crawl away from the assault, but there was nowhere to go.

The fingers withdrew, but Brandon had little time

for relief because instantly, he felt the head of Joe's dick pressing against his ass. Brandon tensed, as if he could lock his roommate out of his hole as easily as he could their room, but Joe wasn't to be denied. He leaned his full weight on Brandon, pinning the smaller man to the counter. Joe pushed his dick in, and the pain was explosive. Brandon let loose with another muffled scream through clenched teeth. He felt woozy, the way he had when he'd gotten drunk for the first time at a frat party earlier in the semester, and he wondered if he were going to pass out from the pain. Part of him wanted to.

But he remained conscious as Joe pulled out and rammed back in repeatedly, picking up speed and force. The pain was constant, but with each thrust, Brandon found himself adapting to it, even beginning to derive some pleasure from it. He gripped the edges of the counter and actually pushed back against Joe's thrusts, taking every inch. Brandon's own dick throbbed and spewed copious amounts of hot cum all over his stomach and the counter without him even touching himself.

He heard Joe grunting and growling close to his ear, and he could tell by the sound that his roommate was also close. Joe pounded him with such ferocity it was as if he wanted to fuse the two of them together, then with a garbled yell, he unloaded. Brandon could feel the cum spurting deep inside him.

Suddenly, the world lit up in a strobe-flash of yellow light. At first, Brandon thought it was in his head, but then he realized it was a pulsing light shining through the window at the front of the store.

With a hiss, Joe pulled out of him with a wet *pop*

and stumbled away. Brandon remained bent over the counter, gasping and mustering up enough strength to stand on his own. He could feel cum and possibly blood leaking from his torn asshole and dribbling down his inner thighs. Finally, he pushed himself away from the counter and then reached down to pull his pants and underwear up over his shaky legs.

He stumbled toward the back exit, and when his foot kicked something across the floor, he felt around and came up with his cell phone. He turned on the flashlight app and discovered the screen had a lightning bolt crack right down the center.

Once outside in the fresh air, he took another moment to lean against the building. Everything had the surreal quality of a dream. What had happened in the old gas station was what he'd been hoping for since he first met Joe, but he'd never truly expected it to happen. A small smile curled his lips, and he continued on around to the front.

A tow truck with a flashing yellow light on the top was parked in front of the Honda, a burly driver hooking chains to the car. Joe was standing nearby, but when he spotted Brandon, he turned and walked toward him. "There you are. The tow got here even faster than expected. He's going to drop us off at the dorm, so we'll be home before you know it."

Brandon still felt a bit dizzy and had trouble adjusting to anything remotely resembling a normal conversation. He just continued forward in silence until he was standing directly in front of his roommate.

"Why you walking so funny?" Joe asked.

After glancing toward the tow truck driver,

Brandon leaned forward and whispered in Joe's ear, "My ass is a little sore."

"What, did you take some massive dump back there or something? I was wondering what was taking you so long."

"It's okay, I don't think the driver can hear us."

Joe frowned at him. "What does it matter if he can? Why are you acting so weird?"

"I think you know."

"I sincerely have no fucking clue what you're talking about, dude."

"Oh, so that's how you want to play this? Just act like it never happened?"

"Act like *what* never happened? If I didn't know you better, I'd swear you went back there and smoked some weed or something."

"You really going to act like you didn't follow me inside the building?"

Joe laughed then reached out and thumped Brandon hard in the chest. "Why would I follow you inside the building? To make love to you or something? In your wildest dreams, buddy! What, you hear a raccoon and get all spooked?"

Now it was Brandon who frowned. Was this some kind of macho tactic, refusing to acknowledge what had happened between the two of them in the dark so that Joe didn't have to face up to it in the light of day? Did he want to get the point across to Brandon this wasn't something he wished to discuss openly or even in private?

Or could it be . . . ?

The truck driver let out a piercing whistle, getting their attention. "Okay fellas, we're ready to roll."

"Come on, weirdo," Joe said, heading back toward the tow truck.

Brandon hesitated before following, his mind a chaotic whirlpool of confusion. Just before he climbed up into the truck, he turned and stared back toward the abandoned gas station. For just an instant, he thought he saw a figure staring out from the other side of the cracked glass, but then it melted into the shadows and was gone as if it had never been there at all.

THE LITTLE BOY WHO LIVED IN THE LIBRARY

AT 2:45 ON the dot, the little boy pushed open the glass door and stepped into the Cherokee County Public Library. Misty Summers smiled from behind the circulation desk, tapping her watch. "Right on time as always. How are you doing, Paul?"

The boy smiled shyly and looked down at his worn-out sneakers. "I'm fine, Miss Summers."

"I told you it's okay for you to call me Misty."

He nodded, still not meeting her gaze, and continued past the desk. She watched him cross in front of the card catalogue, which towered over his small form like a skyscraper, heading for the Children's Corner just beyond Adult Fiction.

Misty watched him go, feeling her usual blend of affection and empathy for the boy. She knew little about him. He didn't talk much, and after six months, all she'd been able to get out of him was his first name and that he was in second grade at Central Elementary, which was a block from the library. Still, she sensed in him a core of loneliness and bashfulness that reminded her of herself as a child.

Glancing over toward the magazine rack to the left,

Misty waited until the young woman putting out the new periodicals glanced her way then motioned her over. She could have called out, but the sign displayed prominently on the desk read: "BE COURTEOUS, BE QUIET". The rules applied to the staff as much as the patrons of the library.

Anna, the Limestone College student who had recently started working at the library part-time, walked over to the desk. "How can I help you, Miss Summers?"

"Do you think you could watch the desk for a moment?"

Anna's eyes widened with a look of almost comical fright. "I've never worked the desk by myself before."

Reaching across the desk, Misty patted the young woman's hand and offered her a reassuring smile. "You'll be fine. I'll only be a moment or two.

Leaving Anna standing rigidly behind the desk, wringing her hands, Misty made her way to the Children's Corner. As usual, she found Paul sitting on a large, green beanbag chair with his face stuck in an oversized children's book. She squatted next to him, but only when she cleared her throat did he look up at her.

"That's one of my favorites," she said, lifting her chin toward the cover of the book he held in front of him like a shield. *One Big Happy Family* by MG Allan, the cover illustration depicting a family which consisted of mother, father, daughter, and son holding hands and grinning from ear to ear. Winding around the family's feet were a Siamese cat and a black-and-white Jack Russell Terrier. Even the cat and dog were grinning.

The boy nodded. "I've read this one a lot. I like it better than Dr. Seuss. If I could choose to live in any book, I'd want it to be this one."

Misty smiled, though in all honesty, she'd never even heard of *One Big Happy Family*. She simply wanted to get the shy boy talking, help him come out of his shell a little bit. "You come in here every day after school and sit here reading until we close. You know the whole point of a library is to check the books out and take them home with you, right?"

"The sign up front says you have to be twelve years old to get a library card. I'm only seven."

"Yes, but your parents could check them out for you. Surely your mom and dad have library cards."

"My mom's dead," the boy said matter-of-factly.

Misty reached up and clutched the thin, silver chain she wore around her neck. "Dear, I'm so sorry."

"It's okay. She died when I was a little baby. You can't miss what you don't remember."

Finding herself at a loss for words, Misty suddenly regretted coming over to engage the boy. The taste of her own foot was sour. "Well, maybe your dad could come by sometime and check some books out for you."

"My dad hates books. He thinks reading is for wimps."

"Oh, well . . . he doesn't mind that you stay here so late every day?"

Paul shrugged, staring down at the pages of the book as if hoping he could fall into the story and escape this awkward conversation.

Misty could relate. She reached for his arm and said, "Well, I'll leave you to your book."

Her fingers brushed the boy's elbow, and he jerked

away with a hiss. The movement caused the sleeve of his shirt to ride up, revealing a large bruise on his upper arm. A large, *hand-shaped* bruise.

"Paul, what happened?" Misty gasped.

The boy quickly tugged his sleeve down to cover the purplish mark circling his flesh like an armband. "Nothing, I fell off the swing at school."

Fell off the swing.

A suffocating dread settled over Misty like a wet blanket, and she found herself remembering other times Paul had come into the library with injuries and the excuses he'd made for them. A black eye from a bicycling accident. A broken finger from slamming his bedroom door on it. A busted lip from falling out of a tree. Having grown up with three rambunctious brothers who were constantly covered in scrapes and bruises and welts, all those explanations had sounded plausible to Misty at the time.

But now . . .

She was almost certain the latest bruise was a handprint, as if someone had grabbed him by the arm and squeezed violently.

"Paul," she said. "Is there anything you want to talk about?"

He shook his head.

"What is your dad's name?"

The boy visibly stiffened. "Why do you want to know?"

"I just thought I might be able to talk to him about enrolling you in our Adventures through Reading Club this summer."

"Doesn't sound like anything he'd be interested in."

"But does it sound like something *you'd* be interested in?"

"Doesn't matter."

Misty found herself at a loss. Paul seemed skittish, and she understood now it was more than simple shyness, and if she pressed too hard, she might ruin any chance that he'd ever confide in her. "I'd still like a chance to talk to your dad. Maybe I can stop by your house sometime. What's your address?"

"My dad says I'm not supposed to tell strangers where I live."

"I'm not a stranger; we see each other every day," Misty said and then put her fingers lightly under his chin so he would look up at her for once. She took a deep breath and finished, "Besides, dads aren't always right."

For the briefest moment, she thought she detected a flicker in his eyes of some hidden pain, a secret rising to the surface of muddy waters, but then it sank back into the depths, and the boy flinched away. "I just want to get back into my book."

She remained on her haunches, watching the boy, unsure what to do. She felt close to getting him to trust her, and as much as she didn't want her suspicions to be true, she had to know.

"Excuse me, Miss Summers."

Misty glanced over her shoulder to find Anna standing nearby, her expression tight and anxious. "What's wrong?"

"There's a lady at the desk who wants to check some books out, but she has a fine on her account. She's vehement that she doesn't owe anything, and I'm just not sure how to handle it."

With a sigh, Misty turned back to Paul. "Listen, I'm going to be up front. If you need to talk about anything, just come get me. Okay?"

He didn't respond, merely stared at the pages with an intensity bordering on obsession.

Reluctantly, Misty stood and followed Anna back to the circulation desk. She wasn't at all surprised to find the difficult patron in question was Nancy Clemmons. She returned her books late on a fairly regular basis, using the afterhours drop box outside, but always argued when asked to pay her fines. Normally, Misty would not budge, insisting Nancy settle her account before checking out any new books, but today, Misty wasn't in the mood. She deleted the charges from the woman's account and let her check out the new Danielle Steel.

"Everything okay with the little boy back there?" Anna asked after they were alone at the desk again.

Misty hesitated, unsure if she should share her concerns. Biting the bullet, she said, "I think his father beats him."

Anna put a hand to her mouth in an almost comical gesture of shock. "My God, how terrible. Did he tell you that?"

"No, but he's always showing up with injuries, and there's something about the way he carries himself and the way he talks about his father that makes me think I'm right."

Some of the horror left the younger woman's face. "But you don't actually *know*."

"Well, no, but I'm worried about him. I was thinking of calling Social Services, have them look into it."

"I wouldn't do that if I were you. I mean, that's a private family affair, and I think people should really mind their own business when it comes to things like that."

Misty snorted an incredulous laugh. "You can't be serious? This is 1987, not 1957. People shouldn't turn a blind eye to abuse. I feel like I have a moral duty to report it."

"You don't even know for sure if there's anything to report; you said so yourself. Try to put yourself in his dad's position. A bunch of strangers show up at your door accusing you of beating your kid. If it turns out you're wrong, you'll be putting him through a lot of grief for nothing."

Misty started to respond but paused. Anna had a point, yet she had to do something. If even a chance existed that Paul's father was hurting him, Misty had to do something. But what?

"Promise me you'll give it some serious thought before calling Social Services," Anna said.

"Okay," Misty agreed. "I'll sleep on it tonight."

Anna nodded then returned to the magazine rack to resume putting out the latest periodicals. Misty turned to the stack of books needing to be checked in, but her mind was elsewhere.

Maybe she didn't have enough to warrant a call to Social Services, but perhaps she'd offer Paul a ride home at closing time, get a look at his home, meet his father if he were there. It would help her make a decision. If the boy refused her offer, she just might leave Anna to close up and follow him.

Anna thought it was none of her business what went on in Paul's home, but Misty had her own scars from childhood and would do what she had to in order to spare the boy the same pain.

⁓↘↙⁓

At five minutes past six, just after Marty Allison left the library with his usual armful of murder mysteries, Anna went to lock the door.

"Wait," Misty said. "Did you see Paul leave?"

The young woman shook her head.

"He must have lost track of time. Let me go get him before you lock up."

Misty hurried back to the Children's Corner, expecting to find Paul sitting on the beanbag chair where she'd last seen him, but instead, all she found was the copy of *One Big Happy Family* lying open on the floor. His absence was odd enough; odder still was that he always put back the books he read before leaving. She checked the restroom even though he couldn't have gotten into it without asking for the key at the circulation desk.

"I can't find him anywhere," she said, coming back to the front of the library.

Anna shrugged. "He probably left a while ago and we didn't see him."

"He always stays until closing, and one of us was at the desk the whole time. I don't know how we could have missed him."

Anna seemed unconvinced, but she helped Misty search the entire library. They did not find the boy.

"He probably slipped out while we were busy with other things," Anna said. "Now if you don't mind, I have a lot of studying to do for a big test in Geometry on Friday. Can we close up and go, please?"

Misty waved her hand at the door. "You go on; I'll finish shelving the books on the cart."

"You sure?" Anna asked, but she was already behind the desk gathering up her purse and jacket.

"Yeah, I'll see you tomorrow."

After Anna left, Misty went back to the Children's Corner, wondering if she'd scared Paul off by asking too many questions. What if he never came back to the library? How would she help him then?

No one appointed you his savior. You let him know you were here if he needed to talk; that's all you can do for now.

She bent to pick up *One Big Happy Family*, closing the book and looking down at its cheerful cover. Mother, father, daughter, and two sons holding hands and grinning from ear to ear.

She placed the book back in its slot on the shelf and walked away.

WAITING FOR THE FALL

DARRELL HOFFMAN SAT in a cushioned rocker on the front porch. Through the open door behind him, he could hear his two daughters talking about him as if he were an inanimate object who couldn't understand them.

They talked of the fact that he still lingered months after the doctors had expected him to have shuffled off this mortal coil as if his continued presence in their lives were a miracle, but the tone of their voices suggested they were more annoyed by this than exalted. He knew the girls loved him, but he had long outlived his usefulness. The rather sizeable inheritance he would leave them both, however . . . now that would be quite useful indeed.

"It's like he's waiting for something," Barbara said. "Like he just won't let go until it happens, whatever *it* is."

Teresa replied, "Do you think he might be waiting for Philip to come see him? I've sent our prodigal brother several emails, but he hasn't responded."

Philip . . . Darrell's only son. While Darrell wouldn't mind seeing his boy—though Philip would be somewhere in his fifties by now, not exactly a boy— he wasn't waiting for that to happen. He and Philip hadn't spoken since his son was twenty and confessed to his father that he was in love with another man. Darrell had said vicious, nasty things he could never take back. No, Philip wouldn't be coming to say goodbye to his old man, and Darrell couldn't say he blamed him.

He would have told his daughters this, but since the stroke at the tail end of winter, his tongue had become a traitor, refusing to obey his commands to create any kind of coherent communication. And the severe arthritis in his hands made written communication difficult as well.

Outlived his usefulness indeed.

In fact, after the stroke, the doctors had predicted he would live less than three weeks. Yet here he was, nearly eight months later, still clinging to a life that no longer wanted him. And if he were to be completely honest, he no longer wanted to live either.

His daughters were right, however, clever girls that they were. He had been waiting for something.

The right corner of his mouth twitched, the closest he could come to a smile, as a gentle wind sent the brittle autumn leaves scurrying across the ground. It looked like a stampede of color, and off to his left, a pile of leaves spiraled into a mini-cyclone. The rustling sound reached his ears, sounding like music, and though he was a nearly ninety-year-old man, severely incapacitated by age and illness, for just a moment, he felt like a kid again.

Autumn. That was what he'd been waiting for. His favorite season since childhood, he couldn't go without experiencing its blazing glory one final time.

In the yard only a few feet from the porch stood a large maple, and he watched as a shower of leaves rained down, creating huge mounds at the base of the trunk.

Inside, his daughters' voices faded as they went deeper into the house. They wouldn't be gone long, however, but maybe he'd have enough time. Gripping the arms of the rocker tightly, ignoring the fiery pain flaring in his knuckles, he pushed himself up to his feet. He wobbled, swaying like a weed caught in the cool breeze, then started shuffling across the porch toward the steps leading down to the lawn.

His left leg dragged along like something dead, but he used what little strength he had left to keep his balance. He clung to the railing as he made his way down the three steps. When he'd first moved into the house in his forties, he had often leapt directly from the porch to the ground, but those days were long gone.

The tree seemed both close and impossibly distant at the same time. His breath came in hitching gasps, and halfway to his destination, he sank to his knees. Not letting this dissuade him, he continued toward the tree in a crawl. The leaves blew around him, prickling at his face as they wafted past, and this urged him on, giving him more fuel for the journey.

He waded through a drift of leaves just beneath the tree and then collapsed, rolling over onto his back. The day was bright, but the branches overhead shielded his eyes from the harsh glare of the sun. All he could see above him were the leaves see-sawing down toward him, landing on his frail body as light as feathers but quickly covering him with their gentle weight. He made no move to dislodge them, wanting to be buried beneath their beauty. He enjoyed the sight of their descent until his vision was blocked by the leaves covering his face. Only then did he close his eyes.

When Barbara and Teresa came to check on Darrell twenty minutes later, they were shocked to find the rocker empty. The search for their father lasted only moments, however, and then Teresa noticed the tip of one of Darrell's plush bedroom slippers poking up from the leaves beneath the maple.

His waiting was over.

TANNER

"GODDAMN THIS THING'S heavy!" Wes growled as we lowered the tanning bed to the floor in the back bedroom, which had previously been used for storage. My "junk room" as Wes had always called it.

I didn't answer him right away, instead leaned on the contraption and tried to catch my breath. I liked to think of myself as being in relatively good shape, but Wes had a point. The tanning bed was damn heavy.

Wes put his back to the wall and crossed his arms over his chest. As usual, he didn't seem to have any idea just how sexy he was, which perhaps made him so sexy. Was that a paradox? "Jesus, Mathew, why didn't you just hire movers?"

"I think we did fine on our own," I said, though my arms and chest ached. "Besides, saved me a lot of money doing it this way."

"You're concerned about saving money? That's humorous coming from the guy who just bought his own personal tanning bed."

I patted the top of the machine. "Hey, I got Tanner here for a bargain."

"You named your tanning bed? I thought guys only did that for their cars and their dicks."

"Both of those are named Hotrod," I said with a

wink. "But seriously, the tanning salon downtown, the Bronze Age, got all new equipment and was selling off the old stuff cheap. I got this for a steal, and considering how much time I've spent at tanning salons the last couple of years, Tanner is going to pay for himself in a week."

"The Bronze Age? Isn't that the place where some old guy died of a heart attack not too long ago?"

"Think he was only in his forties actually."

"Wait a minute, didn't the guy die in one of the tanning beds?"

"I think so, yeah."

Wes backed away from Tanner. "Was it *this one*?"

"I don't know. They were selling off all their old beds, and I didn't specifically ask."

"So you're saying it could be the one the guy died in?"

I laughed before I could stop myself. "What, are you scared it's haunted?"

"No, but it's creepy, like sleeping in someone's death bed."

"You're being a little melodramatic. Besides, they probably junked that one and sold off the rest."

"Yeah, you're probably right," Wes said, but I noted he still kept his distance from Tanner.

"I'm going to strip down and take a bake. You want a turn when I'm done?"

Wes glanced at his watch. "No thanks, I promised my sister I'd come over for dinner tonight."

I didn't wait for an invitation to join him. We'd only been dating a couple of weeks; it was too early for meeting the family. "Well, you're free to use Tanner anytime . . . anytime I'm not using it, that is."

"I think I'll pass. I like my pasty-white skin just fine."

"I like it too." I crossed the room, kissing him and wrapping my arms around him. I was still in that phase where I constantly lusted after his body.

He pulled away as I reached for his swelling crotch, panting as if we'd just moved Tanner again. "I really have to get going; I'm already late. I didn't realize it was going to take so long to move the thing from the back of your truck into the house."

I affected a pout and said, "Come by after?"

"Sure thing."

Another kiss and then he walked from the room. At the door, he paused and turned back. "One good thing about your new tanning bed, it finally gave you a reason to clean up this junk room."

⁓⟍ⱶⱶ⟍⁓

I stripped to my boxer-briefs, rubbed lotion all over my skin, and grabbed the little tanning goggles that would protect my eyes. I climbed into the bed but paused, staring down at my underwear. At the tanning salon, you always had to wear underwear or a bathing suit . . . but I wasn't at a tanning salon. I was in my own home, and if I didn't want tan lines, who was there to stop me?

With a wolf's grin, I quickly yanked off the briefs and tossed them across the room. I felt somewhat naughty, which made my cock plump up to a half-chub. I wasn't exactly what one would call a nudist, but this wasn't the first time I'd walked around naked in my own house.

Stretching out on the bed, I grabbed the top and

pulled it closed, using the inside controls to turn the thing on and adjust the fan at my feet. Wes always said he figured being in a tanning bed must be like being in a coffin, but I never found that to be true. For one, I wasn't entirely closed in; there was a three-inch gap on either side. Also, the thing didn't latch and could be pushed up at any time.

The machine hummed as the lights in the domed top lit up with a soft blue illumination, bathing my body in a soothing warmth. At my feet, the air circulating by the small, round fan crept up my legs like cool, questing fingers climbing up to my crotch.

The thought and the sensation pumped more blood into my cock, and I looked down to see it bobbing and bouncing against my stomach. Beyond that, I saw an interesting optical illusion. The fan was duplicated in the reflective surface of the bed's top, as was the hinged support opening and closing the thing. These two objects and their reflections made it seem like there was a face down there, staring up at me.

Laughing at the silliness of my imagination, I closed my eyes and reveled in the warm light soaking into my skin, roasting me a nice golden brown. The heat felt good, especially combined with the small breeze from the fan, and a pleasant tingling coursed over every inch of my skin. My cock waved around down there like one of those inflatable "mascots" outside certain businesses. Caught up in the wickedness that had overcome me when I'd first discarded my briefs, I reached down and let my fingers trail lightly up and down the length of my shaft, instantly bringing it from semi-rigidity to rock-hard attention.

Biting my plump lower lip, I reached down further and stroked the silky skin of my balls. I shaved them periodically, and right now, they were covered with a light peach-fuzz that seemed to make them even more sensitive. I brought my fingers to my lips and licked the tips, diving back down to rub the moisture into the head of my cock. I was already leaking, and I ran my thumb through this, using it as further lubrication.

Finally I wrapped my hand around the shaft and started pumping my fist up and down. I had a respectable eight inches, slightly curved—"like a banana, but twice as tasty" I was known to say when in a devilish mood—and all my nerve endings seemed to be concentrated right there, ablaze with a pleasurable fire that burned in my groin with a heat more intense than the lights of the tanning bed. Sweat coated my body, drenching me as if I'd just taken a dip in a pool.

My free hand strayed up to my chest and began pinching and teasing my nipples, going from one to the other even as I stroked my cock faster, squeezing hard. A faint feeling of shame hung over me, but I knew that was from all those years tanning at a public salon. This was my own tanning bed, and I could do whatever I wanted in it. However, I held on to that shame because it made what I was doing feel somehow more intense, like having sex in a public place. You know it's wrong, but it only makes the feeling all the more right.

As the pleasure built toward the climax, my free hand left my nipples to grasp my balls, kneading and tugging them. A strangled cry escaped me as cum splattered my stomach and chest, feeling so hot I almost expected to hear it sizzling against my skin.

Some of the sticky mess also got on the tanning bed itself. I'd have to give the thing a good wipe-down later.

I lay panting for a moment, laughing and continuing to yank on my cock even as it softened. Being the recipient of a particularly overactive sex drive, masturbation wasn't anything new for me; I usually pleasured myself at least once a day, but somehow, doing it in the tanning bed added a little extra thrill that made the climax extra powerful. Even now, my body continued to thrum and tingle as if massaged by invisible fingers.

"Thanks, Tanner," I said, reaching up to pat the top, realizing too late I was just smearing more cum across the glass. "You sure know how to show a guy a good time."

—◦|◦—

After that, I started wanking in Tanner a lot. Not an obsessive amount, not like I would call off work just to lie in my tanning bed and rub one out. But I'd spend some time in the bed pleasuring myself almost every day.

My imagination started to run wild. Sometimes it felt like I wasn't alone in there, as if someone I couldn't see was with me, and it was this invisible presence getting me off. Now, I'm not averse to sexual fantasies, but usually I have someone specific in mind. Channing Tatum, Adam Levin, Ricky Gervais—don't judge me, I have an eclectic taste in men. This was different though; it wasn't about the physical body but about the sensations.

About a week after I got Tanner, I was lying in there, stroking myself, and suddenly my hand didn't feel like a hand anymore. It felt like a mouth—hot and wet and tight and hungry. The sensation was so detailed I could practically feel a tongue licking around the head and teeth grazing lightly up and down the length of my meat. The suction was intense, as if the unseen mouth was sucking me like a straw, drawing out all my cum.

When I unloaded, I felt myself being swallowed down to the root as well as fingers rubbing against my puckering ass. I arched my back, and my entire body shuddered as I shot my wad. When I lifted the top of the bed and sat up, I was surprised to find only a slight stickiness on my stomach. It felt like I'd cum buckets.

After that, every wank session in the tanning bed was accompanied by the phantom sensations. A mouth on my cock, hands fondling me, moist lips pressed against mine, even a finger sliding inside my ass and caressing my prostate. For a fantasy of a nonspecific lover, it was remarkably detailed and realistic and always left me drained but satisfied.

❦

"I'm glad that's done," I said, flopping onto the sofa.

Wes sat next to me. "Done? We've got all my stuff moved in, but there's still a ton of unpacking to do."

"Well, that's on you. I opened up my home to you, so it's your responsibility to find space in it for all your belongings."

"You know there's that whole back bedroom."

"You mean Tanner's room?"

"You've been in a relationship with me longer than with the machine."

"Only by a couple of weeks," I said, smiling. "You're not jealous of Tanner, are you?"

"Nah, he could never do this for you."

And then Wes was on his knees tugging at my pants. We were three months into our relationship, taking the somewhat frightening step of living together, but I hadn't mentioned to him the fun I was having in the tanning bed. Silly as it sounded, I felt a little guilty about it. Besides, I figured I was going to be spending a lot less time with Tanner from now on.

No fantasy lover could compare to the feel of Wes's sweet mouth on my cock.

—✺—

For the next month, I didn't use the tanning bed once. All my spare time was spent in bed with Wes. We were still in the newlywed phase, sporting constant boners and using them every chance we got. My tan began to fade, but I didn't care. Tanner was the last thing on my mind.

Then the thing started to malfunction. I would hear a humming from the back bedroom and go in to find that Tanner was turned on, the soft blue glow of the lights leaking out and frosting the room with a cold phosphorescence.

I would turn it off, assuming it was some kind of short in the system, and tell myself I'd get an electrician to look at the machine. Of course, I never did. Since I wasn't using the tanning bed much anymore, it didn't seem like a priority.

"You should get rid of the damn thing," Wes said one night over Chinese takeout.

"Get rid of Tanner? That's crazy talk."

"It's taking up space back there. We could clear it out and turn that back room into a guestroom or something."

"I admit, I haven't done any tanning lately, but these things ebb and flow. I'll get back to it."

"We could make some money. Put it up on Craig's List or even just sell it for scrap."

"We're not junking Tanner. I'll be back in his warm embrace before you know it."

Wes chewed his sweet and sour chicken, holding up his chopsticks as if waiting to catch a fly. "Well, I guess it's better than the spray-on crap."

⁓ˎ◟ˏ⁓

The decision to get rid of Tanner came a week later, on a Sunday.

I'd left Wes sleeping to grab from the grocery store what I needed to make him a big waffle breakfast. I was trying hard to be a good little wife. I was gone no more than half an hour, but when I pulled back into the drive and stepped out of the car, I could hear Wes screaming inside.

The groceries forgotten in the trunk, I dashed into the house, heading for the bedroom but stopping when I realized the screaming was coming from elsewhere.

I followed the screaming, which was punctuated with some kind of pounding, back to Tanner's room.

I came into the room, my lips dipping into a frown as I surveyed the scene. Tanner was turned on, and through the gap, I could see Wes in there, kicking and beating frantically, his body flopping around as if he were being electrocuted, the whole time screaming.

Worried that maybe the short was more serious

than I knew and he was actually being electrocuted, I rushed over, grabbed the top of the tanning bed, and pushed it up. Instantly, Wes slid off the thing and onto the floor, panting as if hyperventilating. He wore only his tighty-whitey underwear, his skin slicked with a mixture of lotion and sweat. The tanning goggles fell off his face and skittered across the floor.

"Are you okay?" I asked, crouching down next to him and grabbing him by the shoulders. "What's wrong? You hurt?"

"I couldn't get out," he gasped.

"What?"

He motioned toward the tanning bed. "The thing locked on me; I couldn't get out."

My concern dissipated as I realized Wes wasn't injured, but my frown deepened. "What are you talking about? Tanner doesn't lock."

"I'm telling you, it locked, I couldn't get it to open back up. I was trapped."

I stood and walked over to the tanning bed, closing it once again. "Look, it doesn't even have a latch. Just opens and closes on these two hinges." I demonstrated by lifting the top again then closing it and lifting it two more times for good measure. "It's impossible to get stuck inside. These things are designed that way."

Wes rose, still shaky on his feet, and backed up until his back hit the wall. "I'm telling you. I woke up when I heard you starting your car. Figured I'd get a shower, but on my way to the bathroom, I heard a buzzing kind of hum from in here. I came in to check it out, and the tanning bed was on. I thought maybe you'd used it before you left and forgot to turn it off again. I was just about to turn it off when I figured what the hell, I'd give it a try. But I wasn't in there five minutes before it started getting way too hot. I tried to turn it off, but the fucking thing wouldn't turn off, so I tried to open the top, and it wouldn't budge. If you hadn't come back when you did, I hate to think what might have happened."

I reached out and hit the OFF switch, and instantly, the humming stopped, and the lights extinguished.

"It wouldn't turn off, and it wouldn't open!" Wes shouted.

"It's okay; I believe you." Although I wasn't entirely sure I did. I thought it was more likely the top of the bed was heavier than he expected, and when it didn't open on his first push, he started to freak out. As for the thing not turning off, Wes had never used any tanning bed before, let alone this one, and with the goggles over his eyes, he had more than likely been hitting the wrong button. Still, I figured it was best to placate him.

"I want you to get rid of that thing," he said, glaring at Tanner as if he thought it was something living and vicious, and perhaps he wanted to take a sledge hammer to it.

"Just calm down a minute and—"

"I said, I want you to get rid of it! Either it goes or I go."

The situation had become so absurd I couldn't help but laugh, which I could tell from Wes' expression was a mistake. "You can't seriously be giving me an ultimatum over a tanning bed."

"I'm just stating the facts. That thing is malfunctioning, and it's dangerous. I want it out of the house."

I paused for a moment but not because I was considering my options. Wes was important to me, and I wasn't going to do anything to lose him. If he wanted me to shave my head and tattoo Latin symbols on my cranium, I might consider it. He was acting irrational and a little crazy, but I loved him. I sighed and said, "Fine, I'll put an ad up on Craig's List tonight."

Behind me, the top of the tanning bed slammed shut.

— ❊ —

I wandered to the back bedroom and placed my hand on the top of Tanner. Roger, the guy who'd answered the ad, would be here in another hour to pick up the machine, and I was feeling a little depressed.

Which was silly. It was just a tanning bed and one I'd owned a relatively short period of time, but I'd certainly had some fun in the thing.

Just thinking about it had my cock springing to attention. I drummed my fingers on the top of the machine, considering. Wes was out, the computers at the plant where he worked had crashed, and they needed him to come in to fix them. Who knew living with an IT guy would be similar to being married to a doctor? I still had an hour before Roger was expected, plenty of time to slip in and wank off.

But Tanner didn't really belong to me anymore; I would be splattering my cum all over someone else's property.

"Fuck it. I'll wipe it down real good," I muttered to myself and started stripping.

Once I was settled in the bed and adjusted the

setting, I wasted no time. I grabbed my meat and started pumping it, my other hand snaking down to rub at my asshole, the very tip of my middle finger probing inside. Sweat slicked my skin, and I felt feverish, only no fever had ever felt this good before.

I had been at it for maybe ten minutes, bringing myself just to the edge of climax then backing off, prolonging the pleasure, when the heat became uncomfortable. Even as I continued stroking my cock, I removed the fingers of my other hand from my ass and reached up to the controls. I attempted to dial down the setting from medium to low, but nothing happened. I tried again with the same lack of result.

Turned out Wes was right. Whatever short caused Tanner to turn itself on occasionally also seemed to be preventing the machine from being turned off. I let my hand fall away from my cock, yet I stayed hard, and a tight squeezing ran up and down the length of the shaft as if I was receiving an expert hand job from my invisible fantasy lover.

Ignoring this, I pressed up on the top of the tanning bed . . . It didn't move. Redoubling my efforts, I pushed harder, the muscles in my arms popping out, but it was as if a great weight lay on top of the tanning bed.

I actually laughed and found myself repeating the words I'd said to Wes the day he'd gotten trapped in the bed. "The thing can't lock. It's impossible to get stuck inside. It's designed that way."

Despite the logic of these arguments, I found myself very much stuck inside Tanner. The blue light intensified to the point where it stung my eyes even through the dark goggles. The glass became so hot, it singed my fingers, and I jerked them away. A safety mechanism was supposed to prevent the temperature from getting over eighty degrees, but it felt well over a hundred.

The fan at my feet began to emit a rumbling noise, which sounded almost like a growl. I glanced down and once again saw that optical illusion of a face, only the face was no longer stationary. It seemed to be moving forward, making its way up my legs toward my crotch, its mouth opening to reveal a yawning black void.

I tried to crawl away, but of course there was nowhere to go. I realized I was still laughing, though the sound was high-pitched with an edge of hysteria. I knew I was panicking and this was probably impairing my judgment, but I placed my hands back on the glass underside despite the heat instantly blistering my skin, and a sizzling, like frying bacon, filled my ears. I tried in vain to free myself.

Suddenly, the phantom mouth swallowed my cock, deep-throating me with a tight suction that wiped away all else, even the pain in my hands. I was licked and suckled and milked, and in only moments, I felt myself unleashing what felt like gallons of cum. It didn't end the assault, however. Even as my cock softened, the sucking and stroking continued unabated. The ecstasy bordered on agony as I was worked back up to a full erection and shot another hot load.

And still it continued.

By my fifth load, it felt like red-hot needles were ripping their way out of my cock instead of semen. Distantly, I heard a knocking at the front door, and I knew it must be Roger. I think I tried to call out, but I was so drained and weak that a breathy croak was all I could manage. After a while, the knocking stopped, the man apparently giving up and going away.

I shot load after load, long after I would have thought I had no more to give. I no longer tried to open the tanning bed because I lacked the strength to even lift my arms. It was so hot inside Tanner, and I was so drenched in sweat it felt like I was melting. I lost track of how many times I came, but I lost a little more of my life force with every load.

Looking down my body, I thought I could detect a hazy form seemingly made of smoke hovering over my crotch, bobbing up and down like the head of an eager lover. My vision grayed around the edges, and I knew I was about to lose consciousness.

My last coherent thought before the darkness consumed me was to wonder if there would be nothing left but a desiccated husk, like a dried up snake skin, when Wes finally found me.

GO TO SLEEPY LITTLE BABY

THE WOMAN SAT in the wooden rocking chair next to the crib, gazing down at the six-month-old baby, which kicked and squirmed and *cooed* up at her. Tracks of dried tears streaked her cheeks, and her eyes brimmed with new tears waiting to be shed.

"Get on with it," said her husband from the doorway of the nursery. "We have to get going."

She looked at him, silently pleading, but he remained unmoved. Finally, she turned back to the baby and started singing in a soft, cracked voice: "Go to sleepy little baby, before the Boogeyman gets you. Mama's gone, Daddy's gone, nobody's here but the baby."

Then she stood, leaned down, and planted a kiss on the child's forehead. Fresh tears fell into the crib before she turned away and fled the room into the hallway.

Her husband waited there, holding out her coat. "We need to go," he said gruffly. "We want to be gone when *he* gets here."

The woman splayed a hand over her belly, three months ripe with a new child. Her fifth. "Must we do this?"

Her husband sighed and then put an arm around her shoulders. "You know this is how it has to be."

"Just one . . . I'd like to be able to keep just one."

Her husband waved his free arm to indicate their home. "Do you want to lose all we have? The luxury we enjoy? Do you want to go back to living in a hovel and scrounging for food?"

She hesitated before she shook her head, crying with renewed vigor. Her voice dripping with shame, she said, "No."

"This is the price we must pay for the blessings *he* has bestowed on us. If we renege on our deal, it all goes away."

He then helped the woman into her coat and led her down the stairs and out of the house.

When they returned two hours later, the crib was empty.

THE FARM

BECKET WAS EXAMINING the oak tree in the front lawn when a Honda Fit pulled onto the gravel drive. He lowered his cell, with which he'd been taking pictures, and waited as the car coasted to a stop next to him. The window rolled down, and an older man with gray-streaked black hair stared at him from behind sunglasses. "Can I help you with something?"

Flashing his most charming smile, Becket said, "Just looking around."

The man in the car removed the sunglasses and squinted at Becket. "Is there some reason you're *looking around* on my property?"

"Yours? I was under the impression no one had lived here in years."

"That was true until I bought the place six months ago."

"Oh, well, that explains it. I thought everything looked so nice, was hard to imagine the property was abandoned."

The man continued to stare at Becket, his expression blank, his lips turned down in a slight frown. He quickly cut his eyes to the oak and then back. "You one of those *Farm* freaks?"

"I'm sorry, what?"

The man sighed. "When I bought this property, I had no idea they'd filmed some cheapie horror flick here thirty years ago. Only found out when people started showing up, wanting to take pictures and babble about *The Farm*. One guy even tried to break into my house."

"I'm no criminal," Becket assured, holding up his hands. "I am a fan of the movie, I admit. In fact, that's the whole reason I came to the States for my vacation."

With a tilt of his head, the man asked, "What's that accent, Australian?"

"New Zealand, actually."

"You mean to tell me you traveled halfway across the globe to visit the filming location of some 80s slasher movie?"

"Not one but several. I'm starting here; then, I'll be heading to North Hollywood to the houses used in *A Nightmare on Elm Street* and *Halloween*. Afterwards, I'm flying to Pittsburg to see the sites of some of the Romero films. I saved up a year to afford this trip."

"This your idea of fun?" the man asked, the corners of his lip flicking upward now.

Becket leaned down, placing his elbows on the edge of the car window. "Well, it's not my *only* idea of fun."

The man laughed. "My name's Victor by the way."

"Nice to meet you, Victor. I'm Becket."

"So who's accompanying you on this gruesome journey?"

"No one, I'm all by my lonesome," Becket said with an affected pout. He was flirting hard, but his instincts told him that Victor was receptive, and it might get his foot in the door, both figuratively and literally. "So how did you know I was a fan of *The Farm* and not just your run-of-the-mill trespasser?"

"You were taking pictures of my tree. The one with the engraving."

"That's right, where newlyweds Judy and Mitch carved their initials inside a heart at the beginning of the movie before the shit hit the fan. I can't believe it's still there after all these years."

"I think some of the visitors keep carving it back out. Honestly, when I first realized I was going to be getting horror fans making pilgrimages out here, I considered just chopping the tree down."

"Why would you want to do that, silly?" Becket said, reaching through the window to slap Victor playfully on the arm. "What you should do is bring out snacks and drinks and start charging."

"Now that's an idea. Of course, I really don't get all that many visitors, just two or three a month."

"Yeah, *The Farm* isn't as well-known as other horror films of its era, but it's personally one of my favorites."

"It's popular enough that I've considered putting a fence around the property. I just don't like people wandering into my yard."

"I am sorry; I honestly didn't think anyone lived here."

"Oh no, I didn't . . . I mean, you seem all right."

"I should get going nonetheless," Becket said, straightening up.

"You don't have to rush off. If you want to wander around a bit and take some more pictures, I guess there's no harm."

"You sure?"

"Absolutely."

"Great. Should I move my car?"

Victor glanced through the windshield to where Becket had parked his rented Kia at the end of the drive. "No, you're fine. There's room for me to park on the other side of you."

"Well, I really appreciate this, Vic. You don't mind if I call you Vic, do you?"

"Um, not at all."

Becket stood there and watched as Victor pulled the car down to the end of the drive. The man got out and opened up the back, where several grocery bags were waiting. Becket picked up the pack at his feet, threw it over his left shoulder, and wandered across to the remnants of an old well, now just a few loose stones lying around and a grate covering the hole in the ground. He took a few pictures as the well featured in a key scene from *The Farm*.

Without being obvious, Becket kept an eye on Victor in his periphery, watching the man as he stood at the back of the car, plastic bags dangling from his hands, staring at Becket in a not-remotely-subtle way. To move things along at a quicker pace, Becket reached down and readjusted himself through his pants.

As if on cue, Victor said, "Hey Becket."

Becket turned and said, "Oh, yes?" as if he'd forgotten Victor was there.

"I've got a proposition for you. If you help me haul these groceries inside, I'll give you a little tour of the house."

Becket turned on his high-wattage smile and walked toward the car. "You've got yourself a deal."

—◦—

They went in through the back, which led directly into the kitchen. Yellow walls, white linoleum, gleaming silver appliances. In the middle of the space was a butcher block island, where Victor indicated they should place the groceries.

Five bags, three carried by Victor and two by Becket. Not exactly a haul which required an extra set of hands, but of course, Becket suspected Victor had another agenda for inviting him inside. Which was fine because so did Becket.

After placing the bags on the island, Becket stood, staring around at his surroundings.

"Look familiar?" Victor asked, placing a carton of milk in the fridge.

"Well, there are a lot of differences. In the movie, the walls were blue, the floor hardwood, the appliances were older, and that island wasn't there. Still, the sink is the same, and the cabinets have been painted over, but I think they are original to the house."

"Wow, how many times have you watched that movie?"

"Too many to count."

As Vincent stowed dried goods in one of the cabinets, he also looked around the room as if it were the first time he'd ever seen it. "Did anything . . . you know, *grisly* happen in the kitchen?"

Becket crossed his arms and tilted his head. "Wait a minute, are you telling me you've never seen *The Farm*?"

"When I first found out the movie was filmed here, I rented it off Amazon Prime and tried to watch it, but after ten minutes, I gave up."

"Come on, it isn't that bad."

"Horror just isn't my thing. I'm more a comedy guy."

"Horror and comedy actually have a lot in common. It's all about the payoff, surprising a reaction out of the audience."

"Well, I prefer that reaction to be laughing instead of screaming."

"Some screaming can be fun," Becket said, enjoying the blush rising in Victor's cheeks. "You know, like on a rollercoaster."

"I don't like rollercoasters either."

Becket nodded. "To answer your question, no, nothing grisly happened in the kitchen. In fact, the only scene that took place in this room was of Judy and Mitch having a quiet breakfast their first morning in the house at a round, glass-topped table sitting by that window in the corner."

Victor bent to put some canned goods in a lower cabinet beside the stove. "Would you like a tour of the rest of the house?"

"Please, I'm dying to get into your bedroom."

Victor straightened up, stammered, then smiled and said, "Let me guess? Something grisly happened in the bedroom?"

"Let's just say our poor Judy had a bad experience in there."

Becket helped Victor put up the rest of the groceries, taking care of the task in a matter of minutes. From the kitchen, they moved into the living room, where Becket pointed out the fireplace where one character from the movie had his head forced into the flames. There was a small guestroom downstairs, but no scenes from the movie had been filmed there, so Becket wasn't overly interested. Up the narrow staircase, to the second floor. The main bedroom was large, with a four-poster bed, a black dresser with attached mirror, a wingback chair in one corner, several floor lamps, but it was the large, mahogany wardrobe in the far corner that drew Becket's attention.

"This is the one from the movie," he said, running his fingers along the scuffed wood.

Victor shrugged. "It's possible. It was here when I moved in. I threw out most of the old furniture, but considering the bedrooms in this house don't have actual closets, I kept the wardrobe."

Becket pulled his phone from his pack again but then paused and looked back at Victor. "Do you mind if I take a few photos inside?"

"Are you going to be posting them online?"

"I was planning to document my trip on Facebook, actually."

Victor seemed to give it some thought, shifting slightly from foot to foot. "I guess it would be okay as long as you don't get anything personal in the shots, like photos or anything."

"Promise," Becket said and snapped pictures of the wardrobe. "I may want to get a shot of the fireplace when we go back downstairs, but I'll avoid the mantel."

"Thanks."

When Becket finished at the wardrobe, he wandered around the room a bit, glancing out the windows, and then stopped by the bed. "This is a lot nicer than where Judy and Mitch slept in the movie."

Victor stood across the bed, and the bulge in his

pants added a fifth poster. "So you said something grisly happened here in the movie but no steamy sex scenes?"

Placing his hands on the mattress, Becket leaned forward. "The movie's big sex scene actually took place out in the barn, up in the hayloft."

"A roll in the hay, huh?" Victor said with a nervous laugh.

"I was only thirteen when I first saw *The Farm*, and that scene gave me my first boner."

Victor laughed again, a girlish twitter, and the bulge seemed to swell even more. When he spoke, his voice trembled. "You wanna see the barn?"

"I thought you'd never ask."

The barn sat about fifty yards back from the house, and it had seen better days. Victor may have invested a lot of money renovating the house, but it seemed he hadn't spent a dime on the barn. The red paint had faded to a sickly pale pink, the color of upset stomachs and diarrhea, and a few boards were missing entirely. The structure leaned to the right, not appreciably but off-kilter enough that it made Becket queasy to look directly at it.

Victor had trouble opening the large double doors, and Becket had to lend a hand. Finally, the doors came loose with a tortured squeak, and the two men walked into the shadowy coolness. The air was stale with a faint odor of manure and livestock, though it had been so long since the structure housed animals the smell was nothing more than the wisp of a memory.

The barn was a wide, open space with empty stalls running the length of the building to either side of them. Overhead, to the right, was the hayloft, a rickety wooden ladder leading up to it. Becket headed that way, but Victor reached out and grabbed his arm.

"I wouldn't. This place isn't exactly structurally sound. Those boards are bound to be rotten, and I'd hate to see you plummet through."

"I appreciate the concern," Becket said, noting that Victor didn't remove his hand right away, letting his touch linger. "Doesn't matter anyway. Down here was where the real money shot took place."

"I thought you said the sex scene was up in the loft."

"It was," Becket said, unshouldering his pack and rummaging through the contents. "But down here is where Mitch got killed."

"Oh yeah, that's right."

Becket glanced up from the pack with a half-smile. "I thought you didn't finish the movie?"

"I didn't, but I've heard plenty about it from the fans. He got stabbed in the throat with a trowel, I heard."

"Actually, it was a handheld garden rake," Becket said, pulling out the three-pronged clawed tool from his pack and bringing it down into Victor's throat, just above the Adam's apple.

It happened so fast, Victor had no time to scream, and his eyes registered confusion rather than fear or pain. He stumbled back, his mouth opening and issuing only a gurgling croak. He reached up as if to grasp the handle of the rake, but then his arms fell limply back by his sides before his legs gave out and he crumpled to the dirt floor, landing on his back.

Becket walked over to Victor's body. Blood bubbled up like crude oil, and Victor's eyes were wide and pleading. Now there was fear and pain in those eyes, but it faded fast, as fast as the blood soaked into the ground underneath him.

"When I found out the house had been bought," Becket said, tilting his head as he stared down at Victor, "I was hoping it would be a married couple so I could also duplicate Judy's death up in the master bedroom. Oh well, guess I can't have everything. I mean, when I get to the locations for *Halloween*, I doubt I'll be so lucky as to find a bunch of babysitters waiting around for me. Still, this is pretty sweet. Makes me feel like I've actually stepped into one of my favorite movies. Thank you for that."

Victor's body began to spasm, his limbs kicking out, and then with a rattling exhale, he went still, his eyes glossed over like marbles, staring up at the rafters but seeing nothing.

Becket leaned forward, grabbed the garden rake, and pulled it out of Victor's throat. He then stowed the bloody tool back in his pack along with the butcher knife and handmade glove with knives for fingers.

After taking a few photos, he left the barn.

THE HIDDEN CEMETERY

"WHERE WE GOING?" Beth asked as they turned onto Pacolet Highway.

From behind the wheel of the Trans Am, Billy glanced at her with a smirking half-smile. "You'll see when we get there."

"You're such a nut," she said, reapplying her favorite shiny pink lip gloss. "I don't know why I ever agreed to go out with you."

"Because you probably heard about what I'm packing."

Beth laughed. "According to Sheryl Harrison, your ego is much bigger than your pecker."

"Sheryl Harrison? That skank *wishes* I'd give her the time of day."

"Oh yeah, maybe that was your brother Ralph she screwed around with."

"Ralphie does get his share of tail, takes after his big brother," Billy said, reaching down to scratch his balls through his jeans. "I just got better taste is all."

Beth reached over and squeezed Billy's leg, high up on the thigh, brushing his bulge with the length of her press-on nails. "You sure know how to flatter a girl. Now, seriously, where you taking me? There's nothing down this road but cows and trailer parks. Not since the roadhouse closed a few years back."

Another of those secretive, mischievous smiles. "Oh there's something else down this road. Something you're gonna wanna see."

"You better not be taking me cow tipping or something lame."

Billy didn't answer, just kept driving. Half a mile later, he flipped on his left blinker and turned onto a narrow road that seemed to have no name. There was barely enough room for one car, trees and shrubbery crowding them on both sides, scratching at the paneling.

"What is this?" Beth asked, glancing out the back windshield at the main road they were leaving behind.

"A surprise. Just be patient; you'll see in a minute."

And she did. Around a sharp curve, the road was bracketed by two crumbling stone columns stretching up about ten feet, a rusted metal arch connecting them at the top. Billy drove under the arch, the headlights spearing through the darkness and revealing a bunch of tombstones.

"Where are we?" Beth whispered.

"The Limestone Cemetery."

"What? I've lived in this town my whole life; I had no idea there was a boneyard back here."

"Not many people do. It's an old place. Don't think nobody gets buried here no more. It's kind of a secret."

He drove around the perimeter of the cemetery, along a gravel road circling the place. It wasn't big, maybe the size of two football fields put together, and the tombstones revealed by the headlights were old, chipped, and crooked, a few of them broken entirely, blocks lying in the overgrown grass. At the backend of the cemetery, he coasted to a stop and cut the lights, only the ghostly green glow of the dash providing any illumination in the car.

"What are we doing here?" Beth said as she unbuckled her seatbelt, turning toward Billy and leaning over slightly to give him a nice view down her shirt. She had a pretty good idea what they were doing here, and she approved.

"Well now, a place like this that almost nobody knows about, all hidden away way the hell out in the middle of nowhere . . . I was just thinking it was the perfect secluded spot to have a little fun."

Beth reached into her purse and rummaged around, finally coming up with a sloppily rolled joint. "A little fun, huh? Like maybe we can smoke this then hop in the backseat for a while?"

Billy's smile widened until it seemed it was going to split his face, and he leaned close to her, speaking in a soft whisper that sent shivers through her body. "Something even more fun."

"What can be more fun than a little weed and fucking?"

Just then, the door behind her was flung open, the dome light coming on and flooding the interior with harsh, yellow light. She felt rough hands grab her and yank her out of the car. She landed on her ass in the gravel, the loose stones slicing into her bare legs as she was dragged backward. She screamed and kicked and flung her hands up and behind her, but she connected with nothing.

Billy had crawled across the front seat of the car and was tumbling out of the passenger's door. "Get this freak off me!" she yelled at him. "Help me!"

He came forward quickly, and she thought whoever her attacker was, he was about to get his ass stomped—

But then she noticed the knife in Billy's hand, just before he swung it forward and buried it deep in her stomach. She opened her mouth to scream again, but he jerked the knife up, and she felt her insides slithering out. The pain was explosive. The world went gray, and she knew no more.

~√~

Billy pulled the knife out, sidestepping the shit-smelling intestines that were unwound at his feet. He looked up at his brother and smiled. "See, Ralphie, I told you this was the perfect secluded spot to have a little fun."

CONNECT WITH THE AUTHOR

Mark Allan Gunnells loves to tell stories. He has since he was a kid, penning one-page tales that were Twilight Zone knockoffs. He likes to think he has gotten a little better since then. He loves reader feedback, and above all he loves telling stories. He lives in Greer, SC, with his husband Craig A. Metcalf.

You can find Mark on Instagram, Twitter, and Facebook

THE END?

Not quite . . .

Be sure to check out the author's *Flowers in a Dumpster* collection, or the *Where the Dead Go to Die* novel, which he co-authored with Aaron Dries.

Or dive into more Tales from the Darkest Depths:

Novels:
Beatrice Beecham's Ship of Shadows: A Supernatural Adventure/Mystery Novel by Dave Jeffery
The Mourner's Cradle: A Widow's Journey by Tommy B. Smith
House of Sighs (with sequel novella) by Aaron Dries
The Third Twin: A Dark Psychological Thriller by Darren Speegle
Aletheia: A Supernatural Thriller by J.S. Breukelaar
The Final Cut by Jasper Bark
Blackwater Val by William Gorman
Pretty Little Dead Girls: A Novel of Murder and Whimsy by Mercedes M. Yardley

Novellas:
A Season in Hell by Kenneth W. Cain
Quiet Places: A Novella of Cosmic Folk Horror by Jasper Bark
The Final Reconciliation by Todd Keisling
Run to Ground by Jasper Bark
Devourer of Souls by Kevin Lucia
Wind Chill by Patrick Rutigliano

Anthologies:

Tales from The Lake Vol.5, edited by Kenneth W. Cain

Fantastic Tales of Terror: History's Darkest Secrets, edited by Eugene Johnson

Welcome to the Show, edited by Doug Murano

Lost Highways: Dark Fictions From the Road, edited by D. Alexander Ward

C.H.U.D. Lives! – A Tribute Anthology

Behold! Oddities, Curiosities and Undefinable Wonders, edited by Doug Murano

Twice Upon an Apocalypse: Lovecraftian Fairy Tales, edited by Rachel Kenley and Scott T. Goudsward

Gutted: Beautiful Horror Stories, edited by Doug Murano and D. Alexander Ward

Children of the Grave

The Outsiders

Short story collections:

Darker Days by Kenneth W. Cain

Dead Reckoning and Other Stories by Dino Parenti

Things You Need by Kevin Lucia

Varying Distances by Darren Speegle

The Ghost Club: Newly Found Tales of Victorian Terror by William Meikle

Ugly Little Things: Collected Horrors by Todd Keisling

Whispered Echoes by Paul F. Olson

The Dark at the End of the Tunnel by Taylor Grant

Where You Live by Gary McMahon

Tricks, Mischief and Mayhem by Daniel I. Russell

Samurai and Other Stories by William Meikle

Stuck On You and Other Prime Cuts by Jasper Bark

Poetry collections:
WAR by Alessandro Manzetti and Marge Simon
Brief Encounters with My Third Eye by Bruce Boston
No Mercy: Dark Poems by Alessandro Manzetti
Eden Underground: Poetry of Darkness by Alessandro Manzetti

If you've ever thought of becoming an author, we'd also like to recommend these non-fiction titles:

It's Alive: Bringing Your Nightmares to Life, edited by Eugene Johnson and Joe Mynhardt
The Dead Stage: The Journey from Page to Stage by Dan Weatherer
Where Nightmares Come From: The Art of Storytelling in the Horror Genre, edited by Joe Mynhardt and Eugene Johnson
Horror 101: The Way Forward, edited by Joe Mynhardt and Emma Audsley
Horror 201: The Silver Scream Vol.1 and *Vol.2*, edited by Joe Mynhardt and Emma Audsley
Modern Mythmakers: 35 interviews with Horror and Science Fiction Writers and Filmmakers by Michael McCarty
Writers On Writing: An Author's Guide Volumes 1,2,3, and 4, edited by Joe Mynhardt. Now also available in a Kindle and paperback omnibus.

Or check out other Crystal Lake Publishing books for more Tales from the Darkest Depths.

Hi readers,

It makes our day to know you reached the end of our book. Thank you so much. This is why we do what we do every single day.

Whether you found the book good or great, we'd love to hear what you thought. Please take a moment to leave a review on Amazon, Goodreads, or anywhere else readers visit. Reviews go a long way to helping a book sell, and will help us to continue publishing quality books. You can also share a photo of yourself holding this book with the hashtag #IGotMyCLPBook!

Thank you again for taking the time to journey with Crystal Lake Publishing.

We are also on . . .

Website:
www.crystallakepub.com

Be sure to sign up for our newsletter and receive three eBooks for free: http://eepurl.com/xfuKP

Books:
http://www.crystallakepub.com/book-table/

Twitter:
https://twitter.com/crystallakepub

Facebook:
https://www.facebook.com/Crystallakepublishing/

Instagram:
https://www.instagram.com/crystal_lake_publishing/

Patreon:
https://www.patreon.com/CLP

Or check out other Crystal Lake Publishing books for more Tales from the Darkest Depths. You can also subscribe to Crystal Lake Classics (http://eepurl.com/dn-1Q9), where you'll receive fortnightly info on all our books, starting all the way back at the beginning, with personal notes on every release. Or follow us on Patreon (https://www.patreon.com/CLP) for behind the scenes access, bonus short stories, polls, interviews, and if you're interested, author support.

With unmatched success since 2012, Crystal Lake Publishing has quickly become one of the world's leading indie publishers of Mystery, Thriller, and Suspense books with a Dark Fiction edge.

Crystal Lake Publishing puts integrity, honor, and respect at the forefront of our operations.

We strive for each book and outreach program that's launched to not only entertain and touch or comment on issues that affect our readers, but also to strengthen and support the Dark Fiction field and its authors.

Not only do we publish authors who are legends in the field and as hardworking as us, but we look for men and women who care about their readers and fellow human beings. We only publish the very best Dark Fiction and look forward to launching many new careers.

We strive to know each and every one of our readers while building personal relationships with our authors, reviewers, bloggers, podcasters, bookstores, and libraries.

Crystal Lake Publishing is and will always be a beacon of what passion and dedication, combined with overwhelming teamwork and respect, can accomplish: unique fiction you can't find anywhere else.

We do not just publish books, we present you worlds within your world, doors within your mind from talented authors who sacrifice so much for a moment of your time.

This is what we believe in. What we stand for. This will be our legacy.

Welcome to Crystal Lake Publishing.

THANK YOU FOR PURCHASING THIS BOOK!